THE QUEEN'S GAME

Raymond Wemmlinger

SAPERE
BOOKS

THE QUEEN'S GAME

Published by Sapere Books.

24 Trafalgar Road, Ilkley, LS29 8HH

saperebooks.com

ISBN: 978-0-85495-845-0

1

1564

"Have your servant take you," Mrs. Parry told me when she gave me permission to be absent from the palace for a while. "The stables can get you a horse with a double saddle." I didn't reply, satisfied that she had so easily believed what I'd told her about wanting to sell to a lady who lived on the Strand a set of gold embroidered handkerchiefs, a New Year's gift I'd decided not to give the queen in favour of another. It was a tale, of course, and I disliked telling them, but today there was no alternative. Mrs. Parry was a friend, and I couldn't risk putting her in danger if my real destination was discovered, and the reason for it. It was likely that I'd need to tell many more tales if my plan was going to succeed.

I did not mention to Mrs. Parry that I intended to go out alone, bringing neither my serving man nor woman. Taking them might put them at risk, when they saw where I went. Besides, I liked walking. My misshapen back seldom bothered me, and I could take exercise like any other court lady. I could also ride a horse alone, with no need of the pillion double saddle Mrs. Parry had suggested. I fulfilled my duties in attendance on the queen easily, and moved effortlessly with the court when it changed residences.

The walk was an easy one, the streets unmuddied and clear of snow on this cold January afternoon. I quickly arrived at the tall, narrow house nestled among the mansions on the Strand. I'd decided to take the precaution of giving a false name, which I told the grey-haired, plainly dressed woman who answered the door. "I'm a relative of one of the families living on the Strand," I said. "I'd like to see the doctor."

Her eyes went to my misshapen shoulders, the left so much lower than the right, visible even through the folds of the heavy, hooded cloak I wore. Its plain wool concealed that it was lined with fur within. It was a remnant of my mother's wardrobe and had once had a gold trim. The trim had been suitable for the Duchess of Suffolk but not for the simple court lady I was, so I'd had it removed.

"I have money," I told the hesitant woman. "I can pay." I'd brought twenty shillings, although I knew from overheard conversations between the women at court it would likely cost only half that. My income from my mother's estate was small, but I also had what the queen paid her attendants, and with careful management I always had enough for expenses. But it clearly wasn't my ability to pay that caused the woman to let me in. She looked back from my shoulders to my face, more sympathetically than at first, for I'd sensed annoyance at being disturbed when the door had first swung open.

"Come in," she said, and ushered me through the hallway into the parlour. On the way, I noticed she wasn't the servant I'd initially thought her, for her dress beneath the apron was of heavy brown velvet, well cut although without lace or ribbons. It was the style favoured by many of the Reformed religion, which I knew the doctor to be, so she was likely his wife or another family member. "There's no fire — we weren't expecting anyone today, because of the weather," she apologised. "But the doctor's room is comfortable, and he should be able to take you right in." I'd guessed there'd be no one else there at that time, and I was relieved to find I'd been right.

She left me alone, and I noticed the good but simple furnishings of the room, not luxurious but telling of wealth. I knew the doctor treated only the wealthiest of patients — nobility living in the nearby Strand mansions, merchants and officials from all over London, and others beyond the city. His reputation had been established long ago, during the reign of my great uncle King Henry, and he'd been brought to the palace to treat the ailments of every sovereign since, except my cousin Queen Mary. During her reign, like so many of Reformed belief, he had gone to the Continent to escape her Catholic policies. There, he'd prospered even more, returning when Mary's sister Elizabeth had come to the throne, and establishing himself in this grand house on the Strand.

The doctor had travelled to Sheen to treat my mother during her last illness, five years ago. I'd all but forgotten him, until I'd recently seen him when he'd been called to treat a sudden illness the queen had been suffering with after arriving at Whitehall. The encounter had been opportune, fitting perfectly with what I'd just decided. I'd remembered that my mother had told me I could trust him, and I'd known at once that he would be the one for me to take the first step with.

The woman returned and took me down the hallway to the doctor's office, where he was standing to greet me. As soon as the door closed behind the woman, he said, "I know who you are, Lady Mary."

He said it quietly, without reproach, and I knew I had nothing to fear from him. He would tell no one of my visit. Then he bowed respectfully, which surprised me, for I wasn't used to it. The queen had made sure everyone knew that I wasn't to be treated as a royal Tudor, even though I had my own claim to the throne.

"It is an honour to meet you, my lady," the doctor added sincerely as he stood up. He was wearing only an off-white doublet of some heavy material and dark breeches. Without the hat and coat he'd worn at the palace, he looked less formidable, and younger, perhaps in his mid-fifties. The hair of his uncovered head was still mostly dark despite being streaked with grey, and his face, although no longer that of a young man, was surprisingly free of lines. "But perhaps I should continue not using your name. You choosing an alias, and coming alone on such a cold day, tells me this visit is unknown to the queen. And we must protect others." He gestured to the door, meaning the woman who'd shown me in. "For the same reason, you must forgive my not offering you the hospitality I should — a cup of wine or refreshment. Doing so might arouse interest. But here, come and warm yourself. You must be frozen from being outside. I assume you walked here from Whitehall, so as to come alone?"

"I did."

He came and drew a chair closer to the fireplace, then helped me off with my cloak. Standing beside him, I felt my shortness, as I usually did around others, for my misshapen back had kept me just below five feet. He was at least a foot taller and seemed even more, because of the gravity his learning and wisdom gave him, something that always impressed me. Although adequate at studies I was no scholar, certainly not what my sister Jane had been. Perhaps it had been her tragic fate, executed at sixteen after a sorry reign as queen for nine days, that had taught me as a seven-year-old that her great learning had not only been useless in preventing her ruin, but had contributed to it. For all that she'd been pressured and manipulated into accepting the crown, pride in her own intellect and wanting to advance the Reformed cause had also motivated her. Had she only waited, until the already too-old Queen Mary had reigned and died, and it had become clear that Queen Elizabeth would never marry, the time for her royal legacy to be used would have come. Now it was possible that my own claim could be advanced.

My cloak off, the doctor draped it over the back of the chair. I could almost feel him studying my shoulders and posture as he placed a flat cushion on the seat for me. Even had I been able to see his face, I doubted it would have showed his scrutiny. Unlike the woman at the door and others meeting me for the first time, his work would have taught him not to visibly react when he encountered the unusual. Certainly, I would have seen nothing of the flickering expression I often saw, when the person immediately tried to conceal their discomfort at my appearance, so as not to offend me. But by now, that polite response was as difficult for me to tolerate as the much less frequent reactions of cruelty or pity.

I sat down, smoothing the skirt of my black woollen dress as I did. It was the plainest I owned, which I had hurriedly changed into from my green court livery when Mrs. Parry had said I could leave. I also wore no hat, having removed my matching green bonnet; I'd known I'd be kept warmer by the hood of my cloak. But now it felt strange for my thick, curling brown hair to be down about my shoulders. I had a fleeting thought that it was unfortunate I couldn't wear it so at court to disguise the imbalance beneath.

The doctor pulled up a chair across from me and sat, studying me. "Your sister has a different hair colour," he commented. "But you have the same fair complexion and blue eyes."

"You've met Catherine," I replied, surprised. I didn't know he had.

9

"In the Tower. I delivered both her sons. She requested me, and the queen agreed. It was an honour to be of assistance to the Grey family. The duke patronised me early on, back when he was Marquis of Dorset. And your mother, not so long ago, which you might remember. Although I don't recall meeting you."

"Then how did you know who I was today?"

"When I was at court two weeks ago, I noticed you among the queen's women."

"It's usually not for the best of reasons I'm noticed there," I said pointedly. "Or anywhere."

He understood what I meant. "I'd already heard you suffered from your condition. You and your sister are discussed. You're important to many people."

"My family succession line is. Both to the Reformers, who would like it to succeed, and to the Catholics, who would not." Immediately, I regretted mentioning politics.

"I'd heard of your condition," he repeated, avoiding the conversational shift. "Without asking anyone at the palace, I concluded it was you — correctly, it would appear. But I'd never seen you before."

"If we'd crossed paths when you visited my mother at Sheen, you wouldn't have noticed it. I was barely fourteen and it was much less pronounced. It had only started to show about a year earlier. Before that, I stood straight and tall."

Involuntarily, my tone had changed, and I quickly stopped speaking. I wouldn't have had anyone thinking I felt sorry for myself. But it was difficult for me to remember I had once been different, with promise of being the tallest of my sisters. It had been a different time, with different hopes and dreams. Even after Jane and my father had been executed, and there'd been suggestions that his treason had excluded Catherine and me from our place in the succession, I'd still thought that one day fate might bring us or our future children to the throne. Both of the political future marriages with leading noblemen that had been planned for us when Jane had become queen had been undone, but there'd still been every hope that in ten or so years politics would have changed and there could be other advantageous matches. But then slowly my body had begun to shift into what it was now. Catherine, five years older, had better fortune and matured into a beautiful woman, although one of strange and distant moods. Her poor judgement had led to a foolish marriage so secretly conducted that it had been impossible to prove its validity, and so it could not be proved that her two sons were legal successors to the throne.

"You should have been taken to England's south coast," the doctor said. "Even better, to Italy or Spain. Conditions like yours always benefit from a milder climate. You said you were thirteen when it began to show?"

"Twelve and a half."

"And so now you are nineteen." Already, he was calculating the extent of how great the changes could have been in that time. Without my having asked, he was starting to do what I had come to him for.

"I need to know if I can bear children."

The silence that followed showed he understood the seriousness of what I'd just said, as well as the dangerousness of it. By marrying secretly without the queen's permission, Catherine had interfered with matters affecting the country and its future. She and her husband had been imprisoned in the Tower as soon as it had been impossible to conceal any longer her being with child. Although now both had been moved to separate detainment with relatives, they remained unforgiven by the queen. A recent attempt to prove the validity of the marriage using the expert opinions of foreign legal scholars had achieved only the punishment of those who'd sought it, and increased the queen's determination for it to remain unrecognised. Many people — including myself — now saw little chance of success in further attempts.

It had been that failure that had prompted my decision to see if I could have a child. But if I did, I would never repeat Catherine's mistakes. To be sure, the queen would object to my marrying anyone, for she feared Catherine and me, remembering her brother had once favoured us and Jane for the throne instead. But even so, any child born would be within a valid marriage and one day might come to the throne. It had been what King Henry had intended by placing me as the sixth woman in the succession, and his son King Edward placing me third. Time had brought changes and now I was second. It was my role in life to pursue it, and I was resolved to try.

The doctor's face showed no surprise at what I'd said, although it seemed that everyone thought poor crouchback Lady Mary Grey would simply fade away unmarried as the years passed. It was surely what the doctor had heard too, in the discussions of me and Catherine he'd mentioned. But it was that very assumption that could help me disguise my plan until a marriage had taken place and the birth of a child achieved.

"I would have to examine you," he said. I was relieved, for I'd wondered if he'd refuse, understanding how politically fraught the ultimate outcome of what he told me could be. He had firsthand knowledge of it, having been to the Tower for Catherine's deliveries.

"I expected as much. I'm prepared for it." I was, although I knew I would dislike it. I'd known it would be necessary before setting out to see him.

He got up, went to the door and opened it, calling a name I couldn't quite make out. Then he looked back at me and said, "My wife assists with women patients here. She is also a midwife, so her opinion is of value. We both have experience of this question, which is a much more frequent one than you might imagine."

"Are your answers reliable?"

"Often, although there is still mystery to it. Much depends on the father also. Often, but not always, his already having children is a good sign."

It was an important point, and one that I hadn't considered. Now, I would, when moving to that part of the plan, if today's outcome was what I hoped for. The husband I chose should be able to father a child, and quickly. Time wouldn't be in our favour in keeping a marriage secret, if the main mistake Catherine made was not to be repeated. Several trustworthy people would need to be present at the wedding, so its validity couldn't be questioned.

The woman came in, looking as though she was already aware of what she'd been called for. The doctor told her to take me to another room and help prepare for them to examine me.

On our way across the hall to it, she said easily, "I lit the stove right after you came in. I thought that an examination might be called for. So, you won't be too uncomfortable. Don't be concerned; they all say it wasn't nearly as difficult as they'd expected. The doctor is a kind, gentle man. And, I'll be right there with you."

"Thank you." There was no need to tell her I wasn't anxious. Compared with the losses and troubles I'd had in my life, it was nothing. I was much more worried that the doctor's answer might be no.

The room was smaller than the other, but with a large window with a screen before it to allow daylight in while still blocking the inside from view. The woman helped me out of my dress and gave me a heavy wrap as I waited in my linen chemise. "We'll reach under it briefly, only where most essential," she told me. "He'll need to touch your entire body to feel the strength of it, but it can be done through the chemise."

The doctor came in and began his work. Expertly and efficiently, he placed his hands on various parts of me as I first stood, and then, with his help, reclined on a table cushioned by a long quilt. His touch was not uncomfortable, nor that of the woman, as they then gently examined my lower parts. Neither spoke or gave any indication of how they found me, which showed a concentration that impressed me.

In a surprisingly short amount of time, they were finished. The doctor then asked me to provide urine and went out. The woman gave me a basin and left me alone while I did so, returning a moment later and helping me dress. Then she brought me back to the other room, telling me the doctor would be right in.

Alone, the anticipation suddenly threatened to become unmanageable, and to calm myself I looked around the room. The doors of a large cabinet near the table that served as a desk had been left open, and inside I could see it was full of books. On the table, one was open, which apparently the doctor had been reading when I'd arrived. It was in German, reminding me of the years he'd spent in that country during Queen Mary's reign.

"Are you a scholar?" he asked as he came in and saw me looking at it.

"No. I don't know German, either. I was taught Latin, French and Spanish."

"Your sister Jane was renowned for her intellect."

I waited before answering, deciding what I could say, as I'd learned to do when speaking of her and her short reign. "She was. But ultimately, not to her benefit. I don't read nearly as much as she did. I feel I've learned more by simply being at court and observing how people are there. Jane's experience of that was limited. Had it not been, perhaps she might not have been led into the mistakes of others around her. But who knows? Being at court taught Catherine nothing."

"What has it taught you?" For the first time, he had a slightly lighter tone of interest, even amusement.

"That being thought insignificant allows you to see things others don't. People aren't so careful when they're dismissive of you. Which is also why I avoid being seen reading or indulging in scholarly pursuits. I don't want to be seen as having Jane's intellect, which she stood out for. Catherine stood out for her beauty. But that's not something I have to try to avoid."

The look on his face showed respect for me. "And what have you seen at court that others have not?"

"The queen isn't likely to ever marry."

He said nothing, yet it was clear the thought of an heir to the throne from a family linked to the Reformers appealed to him. His having left the country rather than turn Catholic showed how strong his belief was. But still, he knew better than to now comment on the possible political consequences of my having a child. "Let us take our seats again," he said.

When we had, he asked more questions. "Your monthly flow is regular?'

"Yes."

"You said your back was straight throughout your childhood?"

"Yes."

"I know none of your immediate family suffered from this. Can you think of any other close relatives, aunts or uncles or cousins, who did?"

"No. There weren't any. There was never anything to suggest I might later become this way."

"That is good. It supports my conclusions." He shifted in his chair. Tensely, I sat forward a little on mine, waiting to hear what my future might bring.

He continued, "There is a wide range of possibilities for childbirth for women with these problems. It depends on the extent to which interior parts have shifted, and whether the body is still strong enough to carry a child to term. It can be very successful, especially with good care. I feel it could be so for you. So does my wife."

I leaned back in my chair, satisfied, as my anxiety vanished. The question that had dominated my thoughts for months had finally been answered. But it was no time for me to relax, for the path that now lay ahead would not be an easy one. "Thank you," I said quietly.

"Don't thank me, Lady Mary. Bearing a child and giving birth successfully is never easy, under the best of circumstances. My strongest recommendation would be for you to remain unmarried. But since you are here, I think that you have already decided otherwise."

"That decision depended on what you told me today. Now I can say yes, I intend to marry."

The doctor held out a hand, indicating that I shouldn't say more. "It's better I don't know of your plans. But one thing I can tell you: if your choice is not made yet — or has not been made by the queen, who I assume must approve it — select a man strong of body, who stands tall, and whose posture is perfect. You seem too wise not to understand that a child draws from both of its parents. Sometimes a deficiency in one can be compensated for by the other."

"I've already given thought to that. I'll continue to. And I intend to pay attention to what you said earlier about a man's already having children being a favourable sign. For a number of reasons, it needs to happen quickly after the marriage."

"Yes," he agreed. "You are surprisingly healthy now. But you can expect further shifting in your body alignments as you age. It's inevitable with this condition. Five years hence you might not have the same chance of success as you do now. Almost certainly not when you're thirty. Youth favours you now."

It was time to go. As he helped me put on my cloak, he said, "Should you conceive, you should be under a doctor's care as soon as you know. I would be pleased to attend you, but the request must come from the queen." The way he said it indicated he already knew it was unlikely he would be brought in so early, if at all.

Instead of calling the woman to see me out, he accompanied me to the front door himself. There, he stopped. "I would offer to get you a coach, or have one of my servants take you, or at least send for a chair. But you wouldn't accept, would you?"

"No, thank you." I pulled my cloak around my head and secured it tightly, bracing myself for the cold. "If I hurry along, I'll be fine."

Once again, I thanked him. The door swung open and I stepped out, pleased to see the Strand was nearly empty. It was only when I was halfway back to the palace that I remembered I'd brought money for payment, but it hadn't been asked for.

Whitehall Palace was quiet when I returned, with evening approaching and most courtiers in their rooms preparing for supper, when everyone tried to look their best. My serving man and woman, a married couple who'd been servants of my mother for years, were waiting in my rooms. Often, I left them alone, and they attended to their routine of seeing to my rooms unobtrusively. At night, the woman slept on a pallet at the foot of my bed, the man on one in the outer room. I didn't have much need of them; I'd kept them mostly because it was expected at court to have them. They were of indeterminate ages, always helpful, polite and respectful, and responsible in their efforts. They were so quiet I usually didn't even know they were there. Once or twice, I'd even forgotten their names.

The woman helped me change into my green livery, then went to tell Mrs. Parry I'd returned and to ask if the queen had any particular requests for the food to be tucked into her bed when she retired, in case she became hungry during the night. It was the one particular task assigned to me, and I performed it diligently, seeing that a basket full of sweetmeats and breads or things more substantial was prepared and sent to her room at whatever palace the court was at. The position was not as prestigious as queen's carver at table, but still distinguishing me from simply being a lady of the outer room. It had been the one sign of my being someone special that the queen had allowed, and I was sure I had Mrs. Parry to thank for it.

Mrs. Parry was one of the queen's most relied-on gentlewomen. She'd been kind to me since I'd first arrived at court three years ago. I'd been called there to attend the queen after Catherine had been sent away, to ensure I didn't become involved in trying to gather support for her. Before that, I'd lived with my mother and then cousins from the non-royal family side. By then, my misshapen condition had been apparent, and the last thing I'd wanted was to have to change my quiet, reclusive life for one at the country's social centre, seen by all. But the queen was not to be refused, and I'd arrived as commanded. The queen had greeted me with polite formality, in no way showing that my mother and she had been first cousins, and the rest of the court had followed her example of reserve, without friendliness. One of the few exceptions had been Mrs. Parry. It had been she who'd stepped forward in the Presence Room that first day as I'd stood uncertainly before the queen, who'd said nothing after her greeting. Everyone in the crowded room had seemed to be staring at me, no doubt thinking of how different I looked to Catherine. "Let me show you to your rooms, Lady Mary," Mrs. Parry had said gently, ushering me away.

Those rooms had turned out to be the same ones that Catherine had occupied at Whitehall. "I don't know whether that pleases you or not," Mrs. Parry had said as we'd gone in. "The queen decided it. There may still be a few things of hers left here. I suppose you might find that comforting, being in a strange place. But then, maybe not, considering how things went for her."

I'd told her it didn't matter, for Catherine and I had never been close. Five years had been too much of an age difference for us to have been companionable when children. After that, she'd been indifferent to me during her rare visits to our mother after Jane's death, when she'd been at court attending queens Mary and Elizabeth. She'd said little to me, and her expressions and manners, always difficult to read, had revealed nothing. From time to time, I'd wondered what she thought of herself, being next in line for the throne. Now, I wondered what she thought of having been displaced, for it was becoming increasingly possible that the queen would never forgive her. Her position was, like mine, one she'd been born into, a central part of who she was. I could barely imagine the emptiness she must now feel without it.

Back in my livery again, I fixed the small green French bonnet to my hair and waited for my servant to return and tell me what foods I should have sent to the queen later. After a few minutes, I was told that she wanted the same as the previous night. Wrapping a velvet shawl around me, I set off for first the kitchen, and then the wine cellar.

I particularly liked the daily visit to the wine cellar, for the long and narrow brick-walled room had an air of mystery about it, as well as being different from the rest of the palace. It was a repository and holding place for wines that had all been delivered from many different foreign lands — France, Spain, Portugal, and even further away. None were from England, because the climate wasn't right for vineyards. The many barrels on their sides on the stillages still seemed to hold a sense of where they'd originated. They were lands I would never visit, and in some way being near them allowed me to feel I had a connection to the rest of Europe.

The steward in charge, who maintained his office outside the cellar, had somehow understood I liked going into it, which wasn't strictly necessary, for most orders were taken and received outside it. But he was a kind older fellow, and whenever he could, he accompanied me to see the latest additions, transported from the ships they'd arrived on — which docked on the Thames below London bridge — and transferred to barges that brought them to the palace. "Three-hundred barrels a year," he'd told me the first time he'd shown me. "And that's only if the queen stays here at Whitehall for her usual time." In addition to the wine, the cellar was always filled with servants and workers, either carrying in new barrels or removing empty ones, and filling orders for various courtiers or preparing the usual daily ones.

But today, the steward was busy. When I asked about him, the assistant I gave my order to instead told me he was concerned that the River Thames was going to freeze over in the cold weather and that there'd then be a problem with the wine deliveries to the palace. He was doing his best to arrange for alternatives, but it was complicated and time-consuming, because every other palace steward with similar responsibilities was doing the same thing. The weather, it seemed, was on everybody's mind — a reminder that it was never possible for any of us to plan further ahead than a few days, and to always be ready for things not to go as expected.

At supper, I saw Mrs. Parry before we both sat down at the long table in the Great Hall where the queen's gentlewomen were assigned. At nearly sixty, her face was still without lines or wrinkles, and she would have looked years younger had it not been for the neatly parted soft white hair showing at the front of her bonnet. Her large blue eyes looked at me with mild interest as she asked if I'd been successful with the handkerchiefs.

It took a moment until I remembered what I'd told her about why I'd wanted to go to the Strand. "Yes," I answered. "The lady bought them."

"Very nice. So now, you have a little more money." She smiled. "With your New Year's gift from the queen, you're becoming wealthy."

She was joking; I was far from it. But the queen had been more generous in her gift to me this year, twenty pounds instead of the ten from the year before. It had surprised me, given her attitude towards those who had last year tried to show the validity of Catherine's marriage. Perhaps it had been intended as a sign of appreciation for my not having become involved and remaining quietly in the background. The New Year's Day exchange of gifts with the queen was regarded as a way of showing one was in favour. But if things went as I was planning, I doubted that I'd be participating at all next year.

One of Mrs. Parry's many responsibilities, making use of her organisational abilities, was supervision of the New Year's gifts. "I meant to tell you, when I was going over the list of this year's gifts with the queen, she commented that she liked yours. So, it was the right choice for you not to give her the handkerchiefs."

It had been a small silver pin, beautifully and intricately designed, used to fasten garments in a decorative way. Like so much else that I owned, it'd been my mother's. Obviously valuable, it would've been too expensive for me to purchase and the queen must have known where it had come from, and that I hadn't parted with it easily.

"Thank you for letting me know." I wasn't sentimental and wouldn't miss it. And my mother, I was sure, would have approved of my using it so. She'd been shrewd and successful at ingratiating herself with each relative on the throne, even after the family calamity. Things might have turned out very differently if she hadn't died before being able to approach the queen about Catherine's marriage. Were she still alive now, she would certainly be helpful in the quest I was now setting out upon. But instead, I'd have to make my own way.

The queen wasn't present at supper, having decided at the last moment to dine in her rooms, with our cousins the Countess of Lennox and her son Lord Darnley. He was rumoured to be in consideration as the queen's recommendation, along with the Earl of Leicester, as a husband for our other cousin Mary Stuart, Queen of Scotland, newly returned there as a widow from France. Much of the women's talk at the table was speculation about that choice. What they carefully avoided commenting upon, knowing how the queen disapproved, was any mention of how it could lead to acknowledgment in the English succession of the Scots queen, who'd been barred from it as a foreigner by King Henry the Eighth. But many Englishmen, including very important ones, were still opposed to it, and I didn't think it would ever happen — especially not if there was another possible heir to the throne here at home.

Everyone in the hall was always more relaxed when the queen was absent, and the other women at the table chatted easily. They were talking mostly about Mary Stuart and what had been heard about her, and comparing and contrasting her household with Queen Elizabeth's. "It's said she has music and dancing every night, and that all the courtiers are expected to participate," one of them said. "She likes cheerfulness around her all the time! And she likes being outside, and insists on her attendants accompanying her on the paths and through the palace gardens. And she's said to like fine dresses, the same as our queen does here, but she'll change several times in one day, which our queen doesn't. Elizabeth is always so busy — she couldn't do that even if she wanted to."

"I wouldn't mind watching the queen wear more of her beautiful clothes," another woman said. "But I wouldn't want to have to go on all the walks outside the palace."

What they were saying held little interest for me, and my thoughts drifted far from the hall as the various courses were served. But my focus returned when I remembered that it was entirely possible that the man who would become my husband might be seated in the room.

2

The cold weather continued into the next days, and the Thames froze over. Ice skaters could be seen from the palace windows, and some of the gentlemen courtiers decided it would be adventurous to try it. Their servants found skates for them, and they went down to the Water Gate, and the queen gave permission for her gentlewomen to go if they wanted to. I wrapped myself in my heavy cloak again and followed them, a short way behind. Although I wouldn't attempt to skate, I wanted to at least stand on the solid ice of the frozen Thames, for it happened rarely, and I might never have the opportunity again. Besides, it was the younger women who were going. My remaining with the middle-aged and older ones, as though I was already one of them, was unappealing to me. I was surprised, for it was the type of thing I'd never cared about.

The Water Gate's gallery waiting room, usually busy with visitors and their entourages, was empty as I passed through, for all comings and goings by the river had been redirected to the other gates. It was also colder than usual, for the floor was set on pilings extending out over the river, and the ice was having an effect. The offices of the porters on both sides were also empty.

A number of the gentlewomen were gathered at the base of the steps, just out on the ice, watching the men racing back and forth on their skates. "The skates are made of animal bones," one was explaining as I descended. "They're attached below the shoes with leather straps. It's out of date for skates, though. I've heard that in Holland they're using metal blades instead."

They barely noticed me as I stepped onto the ice. Beneath my shoes it felt as smooth as a polished floor in the palace, and strangely permanent, although in a few days it would be water again, with floating barges or wherries with passengers approaching or leaving the steps. Beyond the skaters, it was one glassy surface all the way across to Lambeth on the other side.

I heard voices behind me on the steps, and turned to see Lord Darnley coming down, followed by his mother and a servant carrying skates and a small folded stool. The countess was apparently displeased and trying to dissuade him from skating, but to no avail. The gentlewomen beside me, seeing them also, moved off to one side as they reached the ice, where the servant unfolded the stool and set it down.

"Henry, would you please stop this foolishness?" the countess demanded irately as he sat on the stool and lifted a foot for the servant to strap a skate beneath his boot. But he ignored her, darting a look first at the group of women on one side, and then at me on the other.

"Cousin," he greeted aloofly, after an instant's hesitation.

"Cousin," I replied, matching his tone. It was always impossible not to notice how handsome he was, with his angelic fair hair, blue eyes and perfectly shaped face.

The countess had the same colouring as her son. At almost fifty, she was still as beautiful as Lord Darnley was handsome, although she had a more severe quality that might have been due to her age. Hovering over him from behind, she turned to find out who he was acknowledging. Seeing me, she looked surprised, although I couldn't tell whether it was because I was there on the ice, or because her son, who had a reputation for ignoring people, had greeted me. "Hello, Lady Mary," she said, without much interest. "You're not skating, I assume?"

"No, I only wanted to see the frozen river from here."

"See, Henry!" she then said, looking down at him. "Your cousin knows how dangerous it could be to go out on it! She's not behaving like a silly child."

"I'm not a silly child," he said dismissively. He tugged at one of the skates to see if it was fully attached. "The other, now," he told the servant, lifting his other foot.

The countess continued, "Cousins to the queen have a responsibility for preserving themselves! When will you understand you're not the same as everyone else?"

"All my life I've been understanding it."

I almost smiled, sympathising with him. While my grandmother had been a younger sister to King Henry the Eighth, his had been the older, married to King James of Scotland. She'd borne him a son, father of Mary Stuart, and after he'd died she'd married a Scottish earl and given birth to the countess. They'd been barred from the succession by King Henry as Scottish, the same as Mary Stuart. But there were people in England who felt their claim was still strong, because Lord Darnley had been born here. And no one took more pride in that claim than his mother.

"Then why don't you act like it?" she said with frustration, although still in a low voice so the nearby gentlewomen wouldn't hear. As was so often the case, she apparently thought me so insignificant that she didn't care what I heard.

Ignoring her, Lord Darnley stood up, tapped each skate on the ice to check it was secure, and smoothly skated away, like a ship in full sail. Strikingly graceful and athletic, he at once drew the attention of everyone; even the other skaters stopped to watch him. Seeing this, his mother's attitude softened. "He does cut a fine figure," she said, more to herself than me.

Her gaze lingered for a second before she stepped around the stool, preparing to sit, but she lost her balance and began to totter. The servant, watching Lord Darnley skating, didn't notice, so I quickly stepped over to steady her, and gently helped her sit.

"Such foolishness for any of us to be here," she said after she'd caught her breath. "Thank you, Lady Mary. You're stronger than you look." Then her expression changed, and she darted an appraising glance at me. "You enjoy good health?" she asked thoughtfully.

"I do." I had the distinct impression it had occurred to her that I might be able to bear a child. Although the possibility of her speculating about my doing so with her son seemed remote, it was well known that his royal lineage and chances of succeeding to the throne were never far from her thoughts. She was shrewd and perceptive, always alert for any opportunity to advance his cause. Unlike most people, she wouldn't immediately dismiss my royal claim, which through marriage could strengthen her son's. She might have surmised his height and strength were exactly what could best ensure any son of mine wouldn't inherit my condition, and instead look how a king was expected to.

As though confirming my thoughts, she looked back out at him, still the centre of attention as he glided over the ice, and said admiringly, "He looks so strong and impressive, much like his father." But when she then added, "If the earl was here instead of in Scotland, Henry would not be out on that ice today," I remembered they had hopes of a much grander marriage for him, with the Queen of Scots.

It was a marriage the queen might never approve, despite her calculated hints that she would. If not, the countess might see my potential again, as someone the queen might not feel so challenged by. For the present, though, the Queen of Scots would be thought a much better wife for her son than me.

Just past the countess, the gentlewomen were now laughing and talking with some of the gentlemen, while others were playing a game further off on the ice. Feeling different, as usual, and not fitting in, I turned and started to move back towards the steps.

Inside, the Water Gate's waiting room was empty, and I sat down on one of the benches. Although the room was still cold, it was more comfortable than outside, and I found the same relief in its emptiness that I always did in being alone, even though no one on the ice had been snide or unpleasant to me. There had been no deliberately loud whispers of "Crouchback Mary", as there sometimes were when the queen or her senior attendants weren't nearby.

It had taken years for me to understand that the belittling remarks were really attempts to diminish the royalty which I was part of and others were not. The resentment of those who made such remarks was something I doubted the queen was aware of, for none would have dared express it to her, although she, wearing the crown, was surely the most resented of us all. Today, the countess's presence might have been what had prevented it, for unlike me, she and her husband were powerful, with vast estates and a network of contacts in both England and Scotland. No one would make a derogatory remark about the royal family that she might overhear. Or perhaps it had simply been that the courtiers had been too busy enjoying the novelty of the ice to have noticed me.

I was startled from my thoughts by an unexpected sound — a very low sigh, almost a sob — and I saw a man looking out of one of the front windows facing the river. He hadn't been in my line of sight as I'd entered, and since then he'd been so still

I hadn't seen him. He hadn't seen me either, as his back was to me as he stood very close to the large window. When the sigh was repeated, I saw his shoulders heave with it, as though oppressed by some invisible weight. It was odd that the cause of such sadness could be the view of the frolicking skaters on the ice below.

My first inclination was to quietly get up and go into the palace, so as to not cause him the discomfort of knowing he'd been overheard and observed. Before I could, he suddenly turned around, and I recognised Mr. Keyes, the sergeant porter. I should have known it was him immediately, even as he'd stood with his back to me, for he was the tallest man at Whitehall, and possibly even the entire city. The largeness of the window had created the illusion of a more average height, and he wasn't wearing his official hat.

He still hadn't realised anyone else was present. I felt I was intruding, but that it would be worse if I didn't let him know I was there. Before I could decide what to do, he saw me, his face showing surprise and then recognition. "Oh, Lady Mary," he said vaguely. His manner changed a little, becoming official and helpful, but his look of having been quickly awakened from a dream lingered. "I didn't know you were here. I didn't know anyone was."

Although we'd seen each other countless times as I'd passed through the Water Gate with the queen or on other errands, we'd never had reason to converse. It felt strange to now do so, even for a brief exchange, and I didn't know how to begin, especially after witnessing his distress. But out of deference to my position, he said nothing, waiting for me to speak first.

I said, "I was outside, watching the skaters."

He came towards me, and I saw he was without the formal coat with the queen's insignia that he usually wore, or the sword that was normally attached to a belt on his side. He was wearing a slashed sleeveless doublet of some heavy black material, probably wool, over a white shirt showing through the slashes, with the usual white ruff collar above it. His breeches were the same fabric but dark grey, tucked into boots that came all the way up to his knees. As he drew closer, I saw, in a way I never had before, his distinctly featured, clean-shaven face, mostly without lines or wrinkles across his broad forehead. He must have been at least twice my age, in his early forties. But his hair was still thick and dark brown, and his widely spaced eyes, despite having a distant quality, were clear and blue. His appearance favoured his younger years rather than his approaching older ones, an impression enhanced by the sturdiness of his frame, which looked larger and taller as he moved closer to me. And yet he moved with agility, in a way that many such people did not. I stood as he reached me, and found he was at least two feet taller than me.

He stared down at me with a concern that was genuine, if mild. "Lady Mary, the ice can be dangerous for one of your stature. It's good that you're now inside. But if you want to go back out again, please let me accompany you. I have only to fetch my coat."

His voice was deep, as to be expected from his size. It also suggested strength and authority, which he had cause to show from time to time. As Sergeant Porter, he was not only responsible for the gates and entrances to the palace, but for maintaining the peace among all staff who worked there, including the entourages of the courtiers and nobility in residence. He was often called to break up quarrels, some of which had become violent, for which his size was useful. Once, in a palace corridor, I had passed him carrying a drunken malefactor on his back while pulling another along beside him. But he'd spoken to me today in a tone of gentle courtesy.

"No, thank you. I was leaving. I was careful outside and stayed out of the skaters' way. But the river is so rarely frozen and I wanted to see it up close."

"It is a rare experience," he agreed. "I came down here to see it from the window. My rooms are above." Quickly, he gestured towards a staircase I could see through the open door of the office on one side.

I tried to think of something else to say, but couldn't. I wanted to leave, but it seemed it would be rude to do so, since this was the first time we were conversing in any meaningful way. Holding me also was my unexpected interest in his not showing any awareness of my condition, which was usually obvious during my initial encounters with people. It showed in the way they stood or talked, artificial and a little anxious. But Mr. Keyes was behaving differently.

"It's too cold for you to be down here without your coat," I heard myself say.

The remark seemed to startle him. "How kind of you to show concern. People seldom do. I suppose it's my size that makes people think I don't need it. That I can take care of myself."

"You should stay in your office."

"I should," he sighed, "or go and see how the porters are managing the traffic at the other gates. I'm responsible for them, and they must be busier with this gate closed due to the ice." He drew a deep breath. "I should never have come down here at all. I should've known by now it would only make me sad to see them all having such fun on the ice. It's not a place for me, now."

The way he said it was so full of dejection that it confused me, and I didn't know how to respond. Then, to my complete astonishment, he started to weep.

The show of vulnerability, whatever its cause, from one whose position was based on strength and maintaining order in the palace, was shockingly inconsistent with what I — and everyone else — expected of him. Feeling suddenly overwhelmed and no longer caring whether I was discourteous or not, I turned and hurried through the waiting room back into the palace.

When I rejoined the queen's attendants in the outer room of her apartments, Mrs. Parry asked me if I'd seen any of the nobility on the ice.

"The Countess of Lennox and Lord Darnley," I answered. "He cut quite a fine figure when he was skating. Everyone was watching him."

"As usual. It's to be expected, with his good looks." Mrs. Parry sometimes shared thoughts with me that she didn't with the other attendants. "But his character's something of a mystery, isn't it? He's so reserved all the time, no one seems to know what he's really like. Very different from his parents, though, who are always are so clear, even when you feel they're being secretive and planning something ambitious." She laughed good-naturedly. "Which is most of the time, with them. Well, who can blame them for trying to make the most of things?"

"No one." I wondered if anyone ever thought I might have ambitions of my own. It was better if no one did, if my new plan was to have a chance of succeeding. I resolved to stay quietly in the background while someone else drew all the attention. "They've been much in favour with the queen these past months, haven't they? The earl's being allowed to visit his estates in Scotland was a sign of it."

"Oh, yes. And now, they're pressing the queen to allow Lord Darnley to join him." Mrs. Parry leaned a little closer to me and lowered her voice. "You can count on this: if the queen lets him go, he'll end up married to the Queen of Scots. Make no mistake, if that happens, it's because our queen here wants it to. No matter what she says, what pretence she makes about wanting the groom to be the Earl of Leicester, it will be Darnley she wants chosen. And if Queen Mary sees her handsome young cousin in person, I'd wager a wedding will soon follow. No doubt he would cut as fine a figure among the courtiers in Scotland as you say he did today, skating."

I thought again of his sailing smoothly and serenely over the ice, seemingly oblivious to the attention he was attracting. Then I remembered my odd encounter with Mr. Keyes. "I spoke with the sergeant porter when I passed through the waiting room. We've never had a conversation before."

"A very nice man. Everyone likes him. Very responsible, very successful. He's Captain of Sandgate Castle in Kent as well as being Sergeant Porter here, which the last queen appointed him to."

"He seemed sad in a strange way. Is he often so?"

She looked a little surprised. "No, he's usually the opposite, of a rather cheerful disposition. But his wife died half a year ago, so perhaps he was missing her. I haven't noticed much different about him, but he must have difficult days. I don't cross paths with him often."

Her explanation sounded plausible, especially since he'd appeared so lost in his thoughts. "The poor man. I would have stayed longer had I known he needed consoling. Has he children to comfort him?"

"Yes, but I don't know how many. They're in Lewisham, where he comes from."

It wasn't even ten miles away. "Not so far, then. Hopefully he finds solace in them."

Vaguely, she asked, "Was he on the frozen river with everyone else?"

"No, I saw him in the waiting room."

"Thank goodness for that." She smiled and said jokingly, "No matter how solid the ice, a man his size might be too much for it. He's very tall, isn't he?"

"Yes," I replied, reflectively. He was exactly the type of man the doctor on the Strand had told me to seek for a husband. "He certainly is."

A gentlewoman approached and told Mrs. Parry the queen was asking for her. Left alone, I found a seat along the wall in one of my usual places where I wasn't so visible. The room was more crowded now than it had been earlier, most of the courtiers having remained in the palace to avoid the cold. As no reception or event had been planned, their manners were more relaxed, their garments not so grand as when the queen wanted everyone on display before foreign dignitaries or visitors she sought to impress. On those days they would be dressed in colourful finery and carefully arranged about the throne like a beautiful frame that didn't detract from its picture. Conversation would be muted or whispered as all intently observed the queen and her closest attendants for cues as to how to respond as she received her important guests, whether to laugh or gasp in surprise, or sometimes applaud. But today was different, with everyone talking pleasantly and easily. Sitting by myself, undisturbed, it provided exactly the right setting for me to try to quell the anxieties the sudden thought of Mr. Keyes' suitability as a husband had provoked.

The reality of taking such a step seemed daunting, and for the first time since visiting the doctor I doubted I'd be able to.

Some of the young gentlewomen who'd been on the ice earlier returned, their coats and cloaks put away and all wearing the queen's green livery, as I did. About the same age as me, they were at least pretty, some even beautiful. For the first time in years, I felt again a sense of diminishment when I compared myself to them, which had been keen when I'd first arrived. Only when they chose to sit on the other side of the room did my discomfort recede, as did my anxiety. Seeing the women had reminded me that as Mr. Keyes was a widower of still fine appearance and good financial position, the chances of his choosing me for a wife were small indeed. They were even lower when one considered that such a choice would possibly anger the queen. It was going to take a very unusual type of man to marry me — an ambitious one for whom the possibility of fathering a future king or queen of England might be enough. At present, it would be better to assume that Mr. Keyes, who I barely knew, wouldn't be such a man.

The doors to the inner room opened and an usher announced the queen. Everyone stood as she entered, followed by all the gentlewomen of her inner circle, her most frequent companions. Her quick pace indicated that she was merely passing through to the corridor, although she still took time to grace with a smile some of those who stepped out of her way and bowed or curtsied. She was, as always, stunningly dressed, today in a white velvet wide-sleeved gown with grey and silver trim, and an abundance of diamonds, all of which seemed to mirror the winter scene outside the palace. She often wore white, a reminder to all that she remained unmarried, although she was no longer in her twenties. But at thirty-one, her look and manner were youthful, her figure slender and her long red hair thick and lustrous, always arranged to advantage, whether elaborately or down about her shoulders, but either way complimenting her somewhat narrow face and green eyes. Those green eyes held a look of being older, cautious, and watchful, and gave an impression of seeing everything. Today, I had no doubt that even in her brief passage through the room, she had swiftly surveyed it and chosen with great precision who to acknowledge and who to ignore. Myself, as usual, she ignored; most people did.

In an instant, she was gone, the corridor doors closing behind the last of the gentlewomen. Everyone breathed a sigh of relief and sat down again, conversation immediately resuming in a lively manner. The usher who'd announced her dropped his formal manner and said to someone nearby, but so that everyone could hear, "She's gone to play cards with some countess in her suite here. A few of them, I think she said, and a baron or two. No one wants to go out in this weather. She should be gone for a while, so don't bother staying around waiting for her to come back."

There were mild expressions of disappointment, and a woman could be heard saying, "Let's go. This was a waste of time. We came all the way over here in the cold for nothing."

Another replied, "And we were so close to talking to her!"

Almost everyone slowly left. I remained, wishing I could join them, but knowing that with the other attendants, I had to be available should the queen suddenly return. Long hours were often spent thus, in tedious idleness during which the other gentlewomen socialised with each other, or played musical instruments and games, or did embroidery. During most of those times I was fortunate to be given minor things to attend to, usually by Mrs. Parry, like sewing or repairing some valuable accessory that couldn't be given to a servant, which the others might have found belittling. So, I wasn't surprised when she appeared in the still open doorway to the inner rooms, and beckoned for me to join her.

"It's nothing for you to do," she said when she led me further into the queen's apartments. "But there's something I thought you might appreciate seeing." She gave me a look that was mysterious but pleasant. "Were I you, I'd be interested in it."

She took me to the room where she did much of her secretarial and organisation work for the queen. Going to one of the many large cabinets, she removed a key from her belt and unlocked it, then opened an inner drawer and withdrew a small object wrapped in blue cloth. "Come over here so you can see it better," she said, and I followed her to the room's single large window.

She unfolded the cloth but used it to hold a miniature portrait, as though it was too valuable to touch with her bare hands. It was of a beautiful young woman with light brown eyes and curling red-brown hair, her features perfectly shaped and balanced in a way seldom seen.

"Mary, Queen of Scots," Mrs. Parry said. "Have you ever seen her picture before?"

"No." The sudden sight of the image of the cousin I'd always heard so much about was startling and unsettling, not so much because of her beauty, but because of the look of supreme confidence in her expression, even more pronounced than that of our queen.

"I thought you hadn't. There aren't many pictures of her in this country. The queen herself had never seen one, and asked for it to help recommend an English husband." She looked down at it. "It came a while ago, but she doesn't show it to many people. Not too difficult to see why, is it? Mary Stuart's as beautiful as all the reports say she is. And at six feet tall she must be quite stunning in a group, the centre of attention. No, our good queen Bess won't be showing this picture to too many people. And I'd be surprised if Mary and our queen ever end up in the same room."

Something else showed in the portrait — an almost indescribable charm that would draw others, even when it was not in their best interests. It was the look of someone who believed they could always have their way. Involuntarily, I turned away, stepping backward. The contrast between Mary Stuart and myself, and our circumstances, was unbearable, and I could no longer look at her face. She was not only a reigning queen, but a beautiful woman, who would have no difficulty finding her next husband. So favoured by life was she, that she would also no doubt easily conceive a child and successfully give birth. Never before had life seemed so outright unfair to me. My right to the English throne was equal to hers, if not stronger, but she had all the advantages to claim it.

Although I was practiced at not showing my feelings, Mrs. Parry must have sensed them, for she suddenly said, "I'm sorry, I didn't think it would upset you. It was foolish of me not to tell you who it was first — perhaps even to show it to you at all. But I thought you might like to see your own cousin." She was already wrapping the portrait back in its blue cloth.

"Please, don't be sorry. I was merely taken a little by surprise. I know you had the best of intentions, and I do appreciate having had the opportunity to see it." I gestured to the portrait, still in her hands. "It's rather effective, isn't it?"

"Yes. The artist was able to show something of her attitude towards life. She'll always try to get what she wants. Not so different from our own queen here — which is only to be expected, I suppose. They're cousins."

And I am their cousin also, I thought, but I said nothing as I watched her carefully return the portrait to the cabinet.

At supper the queen was once again absent, still at her card game, usually a sign she was winning. Shortly after sitting down, I found I could see Mr. Keyes at his table across the hall, when the many people between us randomly shifted to allow a view. He sat with some of the most popular gentlemen courtiers, a sign he was in favour. During the meal he was very much as Mrs. Parry had described, smiling often, and talking enthusiastically with no sign of the despondency I'd seen earlier. He looked the type of good-tempered, genial man everyone liked because they were so rare. I had met but a few in my life, but my first impressions of them had never been wrong, and they had turned out to be unselfish, without ulterior motives. They had been men who could be trusted.

Very briefly, at one point, our eyes met. But as his turned away, I felt he hadn't really seen me in the first place. He had certainly not been looking at me for the same reasons most people did.

3

The next afternoon, before returning to the queen's apartments after arranging her bedtime food choices in the kitchen and wine cellar, I decided to make a detour to the Water Gate. I had been insensitive to Mr. Keyes by running away so abruptly, and I wanted to apologise, irrespective of any fantasy of marrying him I'd indulged in, which had seemed less and less possible the more I'd thought about it. But even without having understood the cause of his show of sorrow, I should have stayed and offered kind words. I knew their value, having received so few from anyone during my life, especially after I'd started attending the queen in her palaces.

The Water Gate was still closed, despite a thaw having begun, and I assumed Mr. Keyes wouldn't be busy or mind my visit. From where I was, the route there wasn't direct, involving many turns through the palace's maze of corridors. But the queen stayed at Whitehall often, and I'd had the opportunity to learn its plan thoroughly. There was a direct passage to the sergeant porter's apartment, and I chose to try it first instead of the staircase from the waiting room below. Although with the Gate closed it would be empty of travellers, porters might still be about in the offices, and I preferred to avoid them if possible.

When I reached the door, I knocked lightly. I waited to hear footsteps on the other side, but there were none, and after a bit I knocked again. When there was still no response, I considered going back around and downstairs through the waiting room, but began to feel doubts about whether being there at all was such a good idea. Mr. Keyes might become uncomfortable being reminded of his untypical behaviour, and not appreciate the visit.

The corridor was narrow and dark, and the door at its very end was far from the others. It was also cold, and as I stood there, I pulled my shawl closer around me. I was about to turn around and leave, but without even fully deciding to do so, I knocked once more. This time, almost immediately, I heard footsteps in the distance within, becoming louder and stronger as they came nearer. Their heaviness told me it was a large person approaching, and even before the door opened, I knew it would be Mr. Keyes.

"Lady Mary!" he said in surprise as he saw me. He was wearing his belted dark brown coat with the queen's insignia and shiny silver buttons, which came all the way down to his knees, and a broad-brimmed hat of the same colour. Behind him bright late afternoon sunlight flowed out from a nearby room, and past him into the dark hall around me. "I almost didn't hear you knocking from the other room. I was about to go downstairs. I nearly missed you entirely!" Then he seemed to remember who I was and bowed a little awkwardly, removing his hat. "Come in," he said, holding the door open.

Inside, he led me to the sunlit room, which although unexpectedly spacious was comfortably warm because of a large stove positioned against the wall that adjoined the rest of the palace. On one side was a large window overlooking the Thames, opposite the door I'd entered through. It faced another open door directly across the corridor, which led to a bedroom. I'd also seen another large room at the end of the corridor, where the staircase from below would have connected, and which was likely used for official business. The one we were in was his sitting room.

"Please, sit down," he said, going to one of two chairs close to the stove and removing a pile of garments, which he took through the corridor to the bedroom opposite and indifferently threw on the floor. As I sat, I saw that the room around me, although very nicely furnished, was dishevelled, with accumulated items in various places barely out of the way. Everything also smelled of dust, and the window needed to be washed.

Still, as he came back to me, I said politely, "A pleasant room."

"I apologise for the delay in opening the door. I hope you weren't standing out there too long."

"No. Not long at all."

"That entrance is barely used. Almost everyone comes and goes through the waiting room."

"Please, Mr. Keyes, have a seat too." Somehow, any anxiety I'd had over making the visit had vanished as soon as I'd stepped inside. Despite its being unkempt, I liked the room and felt comfortable in it in a way I seldom did in other rooms in the palace.

With a flick of his wrist, he tossed his hat towards a table near the wall, where it landed precisely in the centre. Then he sat in the other chair, which creaked a little under his great frame. Seated so, he felt more approachable to me, his head and eyes much closer to being level with mine. His expression was well balanced and harmonious, but with a touch of distance, as though he held himself half a step back from full engagement with life. But at the same time, I saw he was interested in my presence, and not displeased by it.

"Lady Mary, this visit is an honour for me," he said, sounding a little awed. "Although I can't think what's prompted it." He leaned forward with concern. "I hope you weren't offended by my looking at you at supper last night. If so, I'm sorry! I happened to see you by chance and remembered our encounter earlier. That was the reason my gaze lingered. Nothing else." There had been an earnest urgency in the way he'd said it, as though it were very important for me to know it hadn't been for the usual reason.

It was one of the rare times that I believed it. "I know you weren't looking at my misshape," I said, startling myself. I almost never spoke of it, to anyone.

"I wasn't." He leaned back in his chair, which once again creaked. "People's outsides don't always tell you what's inside. They can have the nicest face and be cruel and selfish. I've learned that through my work keeping the peace in the palace."

It was a simple observation, but the way he said it made it sound like wisdom. No one had ever been kind enough to suggest it applied to me before. I said, "Last night I wasn't even sure you'd seen me. You were so engaged with your table companions. But I too was thinking of having seen you in the afternoon. And that's why I'm here today. I want to apologise."

"Apologise?" He was completely startled and sat up very straight, extending both hands towards me. "For what?"

Suddenly a loud cracking sound reverberated through the room, like a part of the palace was about to fall down. Unnerved, I nearly exclaimed aloud, but Mr. Keyes barely responded. "The thawing ice," he said calmly, pointing to the window. "It's been doing that all day." He smiled reassuringly. "Nothing to be concerned about."

"Thank goodness," I said, and immediately felt foolish for it. "How silly you must think me."

"Not at all. How could you have known what it was? The river freezes so rarely. I'd never heard it here before either, although when it started, I did recognise it from years ago, on a lake far from London. I hadn't thought of it since then." He sighed, and his body seemed to sag in his chair. "This ice has brought back memories for me. Yesterday, right before I saw you, the revellers on the Thames were reminding me of a time when the River Ravensbourne near my home froze. My wife and I had a merry time on it, with our children." He became very still. "Those were good days for us." Although he kept his composure, the grief in his voice was unmistakable. Abruptly, he added, "She's dead now. Gone."

"I know. I'm sorry. I saw you were distressed yesterday, and I shouldn't have left like that. It's what I came to apologise for today. It was selfish and thoughtless of me to have left you so. I know what it is to have death take away those you care about, although I imagine the loss of a spouse must be the worst of all. I'm sorry."

He sat up straight, waving his large hands as though shaking his sadness away. "No, no, I shouldn't have burdened you with this. There was no need for you to come all the way here, or to have felt you needed to. But I'm honoured you did! I won't forget it. You can always come to me if you have need of anything — anything at all! Although I'm sure such a great lady as you already has more than enough friends."

Incredulous, I stared at him, unable to believe I'd heard him correctly. Then I wondered if he might be making fun of me, but I already knew he wasn't the type to. His face showed only admiration and respect. Suddenly, it was too much for me, and I buried my own face in my hands.

With deep concern, he asked, "Whatever is wrong?"

"No one has ever called me a great lady before," I said from behind my hands.

"Lady Mary —"

I still wouldn't remove my hands. "Most often I'm called Crouchback Mary!"

"That is cruel," he said gently.

"You don't have to deny that you've heard it." I took my hands away and looked directly at him, as though to convey I was thoroughly used to it.

"I have," he said with frank plainness. "But it's ignorant as well as cruel for them to say it. Usually hunchbacks are called that, and you're not one — it's only that your shoulders are uneven, and you lean forward a little because of it. I'd guess that if you were out in the fresh air more and took exercise, it might even lessen."

It was almost shocking to hear my condition spoken of in so accepting a manner, rather than in a whispered taunt. He continued, "Don't pay any attention when they call you that. They think it makes them better than you, and they know they're not. Like I said, you're a great lady. I know one when I see one; I've learned from being here at the palace. You can see it right away in people's faces. It's there, in yours."

His words were so foreign to me I had no idea what to say. But from the way he so casually looked away towards the window, I saw he expected no reply. He did, indeed, believe I was a great lady. I felt a completely unfamiliar satisfaction; never before had I encountered flattery. "Thank you," I was finally able to say.

His eyes moved back towards me. "I'm going to put a stop to that name-calling," he said decisively. "It's part of what I do around here, keep the peace. The next time you hear someone say it, you come and tell me right away. I can make sure they never call you that again! Even if it's the queen herself!"

"You mustn't say that, even in jest," I said quickly, "or anything like it, about the queen. I know no one can overhear

46

us here, but you shouldn't get into the habit of it, because you may then say it when someone might hear it. Besides, the queen would never say something like that, or allow it. It's never said when she's nearby."

"Good Queen Bess." He sounded amused. "Can I ask you — what's it like to be her cousin?"

"She never acknowledges I'm anything more than a minor lady attending her."

His forehead furrowed, and his face took on an introspective look I hadn't seen from him yet. "That's telling in itself, isn't it? That she tries to make you less than you are?"

"We shouldn't speak of such things," I said warily. "I have no cause to criticise the queen. She's given me a place here in her household."

He heard my change of tone and understood its meaning. After a moment, he said, "I'm not political, Lady Mary."

"Neither am I." It was time to go, even though I would have liked to stay longer. If we became better friends, I might be able to tell him more about myself. But it was too soon. I stood up, straightening my shawl. "I must go."

He stood as well. "Must you? I have some wine here and was about to offer you a cup."

"If I'm gone too long, I might be missed. Even though I'm usually not noticed by anyone."

He looked around, seeming to see the unkempt condition of the room for the first time. "You must forgive the mess here. Had I expected you, I would have had it attended to. The porters are very good about taking care of it, when I ask them. But I keep forgetting to. It was something my wife used to attend to, you see. My house is on the outskirts of London, not too far, and she would come from time to time to make sure everything here was tidy. Sometimes she would stay for a night

47

or so. She liked it here. It can be very pleasant, with the windows open to the river breezes, especially in the spring. There's no dust, then."

The room did need a thorough cleaning. I wouldn't have mentioned it, but since he had, it gave me an opportunity. "Mr. Keyes, I have two servants who I ask very little of, and they have time. I would very much like to send them here to do some tidying. It shouldn't take more than half a day. I won't even notice they're gone."

"Oh, no, thank you, but I couldn't ask it —"

"You haven't asked. I'm offering."

He still looked hesitant.

"I'd like to do it not only as a gift to you, but to your dear wife also. I think she'd be pleased by it," I added.

It had, of course, been exactly the right thing to say. For an instant, it seemed he might even start to weep again, but he smiled instead. "You are indeed a great lady." He reached into his pocket, produced a ring of keys, and removed one from it. "Here," he said as he gave it to me. "It's to the door you came in through. Have them come when convenient. They can push the key under the door when they leave."

"I'll want to see their work was satisfactory. If you're agreeable, I'll have them bring me the key when they're finished. After I've looked things over, I'll leave the key as you ask when I leave. They can come in the morning and then I'll stop by at this time tomorrow. It's convenient for me because I always have to go to the kitchen and wine cellar for the queen at this time. It's easy for me to tend to my own business before returning."

"So long as you don't spend time lingering over a cup of wine," he said, winking jokingly.

"Perhaps one day when we are friends, I can," I said, returning his smile. "If we become so. I hope we do. Contrary to what you think, I have few. No one in the palace here, or anywhere, would agree I am the 'great lady' you so kindly called me. No one is interested in befriending me."

"The greater the loss for them, then."

He walked me to the door, which creaked as he opened it. We said goodbye, and I stepped out into the corridor. As the door swung shut behind me, the light from the room receded and then vanished, and in the cold darkness I felt unusually alone.

That night, after the queen retired and I returned to my rooms, my servants listened with surprised interest when I told them what they were to do the next day. "Take as much time as you need, which may be a while. I saw one of the rooms today, and it was a mess. The poor man's wife died a while ago and they haven't been properly attended to since then. He said the porters have been seeing to them, but clearly not very effectively. So, we must do what we can to help. I don't expect he'll be there, but if he is, try not to disturb him. And certainly don't take any money from him, if he offers it. It's a gift, from me. I'll pay you a little extra for it."

The curious expressions on both their faces showed I should say more. "I barely know him, and yesterday was the first time we ever spoke. Mrs. Parry's told me a little about him. It's our Christian duty to help a friend when we can."

It then occurred to me that they likely already knew him. I asked, and they told me that all the staff at Whitehall did. They also said he was fair when called to resolve disputes, and was well liked by everyone.

I gave them the key, saying one of them should bring it to me when they were finished. "I'm not sure where we'll be with the queen, but you can find out. Tell the guard at the door to have a groom come and get me, and I'll come out for it. Then I'll go and give it to Mr. Keyes on my way back from the kitchen." It was a way of letting them know I'd be viewing their work, and that it had better be satisfactory.

The next day, they finished earlier than I expected, and by late morning I received the key back from them. Surprising feelings of disappointment came over me with the thought that I should return it to Mr. Keyes at midday in the Great Hall, but when he wasn't there — presumably held up by some official responsibility — I was pleased I still had reason to visit his rooms. Later that afternoon, I hurried through my trips to the kitchen and wine cellar, then made my way there.

I knocked lightly on the door, and when there was no answer, I used the key and entered, immediately smelling the scent of the rosemary and other herbs from the cleaning. It was the same as in my own rooms, creating a sense of familiarity that was unusual in a place I'd only been once before. Inside, beneath the herbs, it was easy to tell all the windows had been open and the rooms filled with fresh air. In the parlour, the large window had been washed, and the quality of the afternoon light in the room seemed clearer, allowing more distinct visibility. The dust was all gone, and the clutter that had been in the corners and on the tables had been removed, now contained now in a large trunk off to one side that my servants had told me they'd got from the porters below. The stove, candle holders, lamps and furniture had all been polished. The feeling of the entire room was of new clarity and energy.

For the first time I went into the bedroom, which had a typical canopied bed, but of a rather simple unornamented design, although the mattress and featherbed looked thick enough for comfort, and the drapes and cover were velvet. My servants had done their work on it also, and it was free of dust and very lightly scented with herbs. Fortunately, they had told me, they had found clean linens in one of the three cupboards in the room, and had consigned the used ones to the same pile of garments they had delivered to the great palace laundry, arranging for it to be returned to the porters several days hence. The single window in the room had also been washed and with its shutters pulled back allowed another view of the Thames, from a different direction.

Satisfied, I went back out through the corridor to the large front room. It was plainly furnished, with only a heavy oak table and benches, and chairs at either end. As expected, the staircase from below opened on one side, but what I hadn't thought to see was that it also continued further upward to the roof. I'd approached the Water Gate many times on the river, and seen the decorative latticework along the top, but I only now understood it contained some open walkway or roof deck within.

From the staircase, I could hear voices from the office below, where the porters, not busy because the gate was still closed, would be gathered. It took only a minute for me to see that the room had been thoroughly attended to, and I went back to the corridor, intending to leave. But as I passed the parlour door I hesitated, then entered it again, this time not to assess its condition but instead seeking an impression of the man who lived in it. There had been pictures on one wall that I hadn't looked at closely yet, and a few decorative items that stood out more prominently now that the surrounding clutter had been removed.

Even in the few minutes since I'd been there, the late afternoon light had begun to fade and now looked more soothing. But everything in the room was still clear, and I went first to the three pictures displayed together on a wall. All were small, about a foot square with carved oak frames, and were drawings on paper, without colour but detailed. Most striking was one of a still pretty middle-aged woman with a white headdress and two neat strips of straight, dark hair showing on either side of her kind but pensive face. Her large, gentle eyes looked directly out from the portrait. Even in the fading light, it was clear she was someone for whom integrity and fairness would be important. Immediately, I was sure she had been Mr. Keyes' wife. I wondered who could have drawn her portrait, and the two pictures beside it — one of a wide half-timbered mansion, the other a landscape of what could have been a deep garden. Somehow, I knew Mr. Keyes hadn't been the artist, for there was a delicacy and precision to all three drawings that felt inconsistent with his size and very deliberate movements. Although he was likely patient in dealing with others, I believed he would find it tedious to labour over drawings. But he clearly still appreciated them. If the woman in the portrait was his wife, the other two pictures might be of his home, which Mrs. Parry had said was in Lewisham. I knew that many wealthy merchants and members of the minor nobility had fine homes there.

Turning away from the pictures, my attention was drawn to a very solid-looking table with two elaborately carved chairs, different from those we'd sat on during my previous visit. There was a candelabra on the table, with fresh expensive beeswax candles, their newness suggesting my servants had provided them that morning. Next to it was a pewter tankard with a soldier or some type of military man engraved on it, and a small wooden box, foreign-looking in style, as though from the Orient. Interested, I slid it forward on the table, and when I saw the lid could be easily removed, I did so.

Inside was a deck of paperboard playing cards. Picking them up, I looked at a few and saw the numbers of the various suits were shown by arrows and knives and other hunting equipment. The deck was slightly worn, as though the cards were used often.

Although my parents had been great card players, they'd seen my sister Jane's contempt for it and Catherine's disinterest, and so hadn't even tried to teach me. After my father had died, my mother had continued playing with her frequent guests, and occasionally with Queen Mary, when she'd visited the palace. At home, she would play with her attendants, sometimes for long hours, drawing compliments on her skill. Clearly, she'd enjoyed it. But there had been one time shortly before she'd died when I'd overheard the servants agreeing that she used cardplaying as a way of not thinking about things she didn't want to.

Every time my mother had returned from visiting the palace, the card games had been played for particularly long stretches of time. She'd been as skilled in her playing as she'd been in reestablishing favour after Queen Mary had executed Jane and my father, but underneath she must have suffered for it. Even so, as I now held the deck in my hands, I could admire the fact that she'd played so effectively in such a difficult game. The cards she'd left to Catherine had been good ones, but foolishly wasted by her. Now that they were in my hands, the same mistakes would not be repeated.

There was a sound behind me, and I turned to see Mr. Keyes in the doorway. I'd been so lost in my thoughts that I hadn't heard him approaching in the corridor.

"The porters told me they heard someone here again," he said, smiling as he joined me beside the table. "I thought your servants might have returned, and I wanted to pay them for their excellent work. They'd already left before I came up this morning and saw everything they'd done. And in so short a time! I was going to thank you when I saw you in the Great Hall at noon, but I was called to one of the other gates right before. There's a lot of confusion with the river gate still closed." He offered me some coins. "Could you give them this, with my gratitude?"

"No. It was a gift. My gift."

"Somehow, I'm not surprised by your refusing," he said in a very resigned but complimentary way. "And I already know continuing to ask won't make a difference." He dropped the coins into the pocket of his coat.

"It won't," I said with finality. "I came to see that what they'd done was sufficient, and to return your key."

"More than sufficient. It's excellent, as I said. It's been months since these rooms have been in such good shape." He looked down at the cards, which I'd continued holding. "Do you play?"

Immediately, I hurried to put them back in their box. "Please forgive me. I was intrigued by this container. I hope I didn't overstep by taking the cards out."

"Not at all."

I replaced the lid and slid it away on the table, then folded my hands together and looked up at him. "I don't know how to play. But my parents did. They played all the time."

"I can show you, if you'd like."

Thinking of myself sitting at a game, shrewdly calculating which cards to hold or release to the thrill or dejection of the other players, was nearly unimaginable. "I couldn't impose on your time. I'm not sure I'd be any good at it, anyway."

"On the contrary, I think you might be."

"I doubt it," I replied, though there was a genuine quality about Mr Keyes that made what he said convincing.

"The offer stands, should you change your mind. We could find a convenient time, when the queen doesn't require your service."

"Thank you. I'll remember it. I should be getting back to the queen now." I was ready to leave, but his manner had given me confidence enough to ask about the framed pictures on the wall. "Before I go, would you mind if I ask about these?" I went over and pointed to them. "They're quite beautiful. Whoever the artist is has talent."

I looked back at him in time to see him blink a few times, and I thought there might be tears. "I'm sorry —" I began to say, but he stopped me.

"No, no," he said, coming up beside me. "I like that you've asked about them, so very much."

"This woman's face shows a very fine person. Was she Mrs. Keyes?"

"Yes. And she was what you say, in so many ways. I was fortunate in my marriage." He spoke with fondness. "The house is my home in Lewisham; the garden is behind it. It's rather a large place, with room for many servants and a barn. My children live there now, the younger ones cared for by the older, and my unmarried brother and sister. They all like it very much. One son and daughter should be marrying in a few years, but they're so fond of the place I expect they'll be staying there, with their spouses. I hope so. It would be nice to hear the sound of babies in the house again. For now, the dogs and other pets suffice."

I almost replied that if he remarried, he might have more children of his own, but I stopped myself. "The artist had talent," I said instead.

"That was my wife. She even drew her own image, using a polished mirror. It's a good likeness."

I looked again at the kindly expression in the eyes. "There's more here than a simple reflection of a face. She must have known her inner self."

Beside me, he stood very still. Then, he said, "I miss her."

"Of course. How could you not?"

Instead of answering, he only sighed.

It was time for me to go. I removed the key from my pocket and offered it to him. For no apparent reason, he hesitated before taking it.

At the door, he thanked me again. "I hope that from now on you will count me a friend, Lady Mary. And remember: playing cards is something you might be very good at."

4

For the following week, and the one after, Mr. Keyes and I saw and politely acknowledged each other in the Great Hall, but not otherwise. The weather improved and it was announced that the Water Gate was open again. I assumed it was as busy as usual, and taking up his time. Meanwhile, I was absorbing what had passed between us, trying to decide whether I really wanted to pursue my plan with him. It had all happened quickly, and I knew I had to be certain every step of the way. But I'd found no one else with the remotest possibility of becoming my husband among the various courtiers and officials in the palace. My circle of acquaintances was too small to provide other options, and there was no way I could ask anyone for suggestions from around London or elsewhere, as was frequently done when marriages were arranged.

As the days passed, I thought things over, although I knew such delaying wasn't wise, for several reasons. The doctor had told me that with my condition, time was against my being able to successfully carry and give birth to a child. Also, just from my short visits with Mr. Keyes, I already felt it was more than likely he would soon start seeking a second wife. He'd enjoyed being married, and I'd heard that those who had were quickest to marry again. And equally important was the fact that sooner or later, the queen would move on to one of her other palaces, and I'd accompany her, but since Mr. Keyes was Sergeant Porter at Whitehall, he wouldn't. There were as yet no announcements or even signs of a possible move, the queen seeming quite comfortable to stay where she was for the immediate future. But eventually there would be a change, and if I wanted to proceed with Mr. Keyes, I'd have to decide before it and take steps towards our marriage.

Despite the improved weather, the queen didn't venture out of the palace, taking her air and exercise in Whitehall's large central garden. A few times, she shifted her daily appearances and meetings to different rooms, for what Mrs. Parry said was simple variety. She had many visitors, who sometimes arrived with large entourages, most of whom would then occupy halls and corridors outside of the reception rooms. Bored while they waited, those attendants often became boisterous, sometimes from overindulging in the palace wine served to them. I avoided them when I could, especially on my trips to and from the kitchen and wine cellar. I found circuitous routes, occasionally through little-used servants' passages.

One afternoon near the end of January I was in a seldom used corridor, when I heard a strange sound, almost a cry, from behind a closed door. I knew it led to a spacious room that the queen had been receiving guests in earlier in the month, but had since moved on from. Wondering if someone had accidentally become locked inside and was now in distress, I stopped and tried the door, which opened.

The large empty room was bright enough in the late afternoon sunlight for me to see a small puppy in its centre, who'd heard the door open and was staring at me. In an instant it came bounding across the floor towards me, tail wagging. I liked dogs and was used to them, my parents having been as enthusiastic about hunting as they'd been about cardplaying. Even before the puppy reached me, I recognised it as a greyhound, which was favoured by the nobility and sometimes kept in their palace suites, along with smaller dogs. But, as I avoided their owners, they were dogs I never went near.

"Are you in here all alone, little thing?" I asked gently, stepping forward as it approached me.

"No," came a voice from the across the room. It was Lord Darnley, sitting in a very relaxed manner in the large chair that served as a throne when the queen was there.

I'd been about to bend down to pet the puppy, but stopped, startled by my cousin's unexpected presence. "I heard a noise as I passed," I offered in explanation. "I only looked in to see if there was a problem." I began to turn to leave.

"Don't go." He got up and moved towards me.

"I couldn't if I wanted to," I replied, for the puppy was now biting into the hem of my dress.

"He's playing. That's why I brought him in here, so he could play and run about. I knew no one else would be here."

"I didn't see you at first, sitting in the queen's chair. I don't look at it if she's not present, because it's always empty." Usually, I never commented on people's behaviour, but this time, distracted by the carefree charm of the little animal still holding onto my dress, I did. "You shouldn't have been sitting in it. Someone might make more out of it."

"No doubt you see yourself sitting in it instead?" he asked snidely as he reached me.

The reply was unexpected, even though I knew his reputation for unfriendliness. "Of course not!" I frowned at him disapprovingly. "No one imagines I could ever be queen, and neither do I. You shouldn't say things like that. It might make trouble for me if anyone heard you saying it."

"No one else is here," he said, not caring.

I was prevented from becoming angrier by an endearing little growl from the puppy. "You do things you shouldn't, as well," I said. "You're fortunate it was only me who came in. You shouldn't have been sitting in the queen's chair. You wouldn't have been, if your mother was here."

He laughed dismissively. "But she's not, is she? And you won't tell her. You won't tell anyone. You've very good at making yourself invisible around here."

He sounded critical in a way that was terribly unfair, causing me to drop my usual reserve about my appearance. "You'd try to go unnoticed as well, if you looked like me! But I don't suppose that's something you could ever understand. You must know how handsome you are! Your appearance is admired by all."

Very quickly, something like resentment replaced the remote expression in his blue eyes, then vanished. "I wish I did look like you," he said tonelessly.

It seemed an impossible thing to say, and I almost thought he might have taken leave of his senses. "You have no idea —" I began, but stopped when he suddenly knelt down and pulled the puppy away from my dress. Sitting back on his lower legs, he held it close against his dark green doublet, allowing it to lightly chew the slender fingers of one of his hands.

"I didn't mean what you thought I did," he said abruptly, avoiding facing me. "About why you make yourself invisible. I only meant that you know how to play the game. You avoid danger and entanglements. You prevent people from using you."

He was trying to apologise, although with a veneer of offence at having his comment misunderstood. He wasn't one who would easily say he was sorry to anyone. For what it was worth, I saw I should appreciate it. "You wouldn't like having nobody ever seeing you," I said. "You don't know how it is for me. People seeing you is part of who you are."

"They see what they want to see. Not me." He half looked up at me, then down at the puppy again. "At least then they might leave me alone. That would be a welcome relief from all these expectations!"

"Expectations? We're both Tudors. We were born to contend with them. Be grateful you're thought capable of it. No one sees me so."

He didn't reply, but his silence spoke of an isolation that perhaps exceeded my own, for he clearly despised almost everyone, which I did not. In talking to me, he was letting me know I was one of the few he did not hold in such contempt. As I watched him playing with the puppy, rolling it on the floor as it continued to try to bite his fingers, I decided that his situation was more difficult than mine. His parents, politicians, and even the queen were making choices for him as though he were a mere puppet. My choices, at least, were my own — or would be.

I knelt down opposite him, to see the puppy better. "He's a greyhound, isn't he? I can tell by the colour and shape of his head. He'll grow up to be fast and alert, if his playfulness is any sign. He'll be a great companion."

"It's not easy having him here. He was a gift from the French ambassador. My mother wasn't very pleased, but I keep him mostly in my room, away from her. He'd be better off if we could go to one of our houses, but since my father is in Scotland the queen wants us in the palace. So, I have to find places here where he can run about." He looked at me questioningly. "You don't have dogs, do you?"

"No. But I like them very much." I reached over and touched the puppy's head.

"Your sister had them, didn't she? Dogs, and monkeys. Catherine, I mean — the one who's banished now."

"Yes, but I never saw them. The queen didn't bring me here until after she had — left."

"She could have learned a thing or two from you about how to be invisible."

"No, she wasn't visible enough. She didn't have enough people see her get married for it to be valid."

"The one who did was murdered because of it." He suddenly removed his hands from the puppy and sat completely still, as though some danger confronted him. Then he quickly stood up and stared beyond me, like he was contemplating something troubling.

The puppy got up, stretched, and trotted away, apparently bored with us and eager to explore other parts of the room. I stood as well but said nothing, unsure if I should. I'd heard it whispered that Lady Jane Seymour might have been murdered to prevent Catherine's son being acknowledged as heir to the throne, but no one knew for sure. "That's not certain," I finally said.

"I'm certain." Lord Darnley sounded vague and distant. "There were too many people who wanted something different. It was a less obvious solution than poisoning your sister or new nephew outright, and it wasn't a permanent removal of them. The queen would have been angry if they'd been taken out of the game entirely. The way it is now, she still has an illusion of control over the succession."

"She'll never forgive Catherine. She'll never let her return. And she'll never chose her son to succeed her."

He focused on my face. "She wants me to marry the Queen of Scotland. She's not saying it, but she does. That's the real reason my father's in Scotland, not to look after our estates there, like everyone's being told. If we marry, our two claims to the throne will be combined into only one — less complicated for her to manoeuvre. It gives the Catholics less opportunity to work for the succession from different angles. So, I'm to be the lamb sent off to the slaughter."

There was disdain in his voice. I asked slowly, "You wouldn't want to be a king? Of Scotland, and then here?"

"Since birth I've been taught to. I have a claim to both thrones, you know. All my life I've been hearing it. Now, I don't even know what I myself want anymore. But one thing I do know is that Mary Stuart is said to have murdered people. She may even have had a hand in what happened here to Lady Jane Seymour."

I half lifted a hand, as though to stop him. "I told you before: you say things you shouldn't."

"And I told you before: I know you won't repeat it. Besides, I haven't ever spoken of it to anyone before. But I'm thinking about all of it more now, because I have to, in case the queen does send me to Scotland. It's best for me if I'm prepared for what I may find there. I know nothing about what goes on in those palaces, like I do the English ones. My father is useless; he's something of a fool. My mother certainly won't be allowed to go with me. The queen has to be careful about the old girl. She knows she can think and plan, and she's ambitious."

I wanted to say that he needn't be so frightened of what might be ahead of him in Scotland, since his important status could protect him as it had Catherine. But I didn't, because direct acknowledgment of his fear was likely something his pride wouldn't appreciate. It was also entirely possible his concerns were unfounded. It was difficult to believe such danger could come from the beautiful young woman in the portrait of Mary Stuart that Mrs. Parry had shown me.

The puppy suddenly came running back, eager for our attention again. Lord Darnley, appearing relieved to return to the present moment, seized it and held it closely. More to himself than me, he said, "Wouldn't it be wonderful to live like everyone else? Having a home with as many dogs as you liked? Where everything wasn't so important all the time?"

I didn't agree, and although I didn't say so, he must have seen it from my face, for he then said quickly, "But perhaps not. Who wouldn't want to have a throne, or the chance for it?" I knew then that no matter how ambivalent he might be at times, he would in the end remember who he was, and make the most of it.

"I must go," I said. "Thank you for showing me your puppy. He's a fine little thing."

"Do you mind being at the queen's beck and call, like a servant? At least I don't have to do that."

He was being unpleasant again, but I wasn't going to be drawn into it. "Your mother takes her place in the rotation serving the queen as well. It's an honour. She doesn't seem to mind it."

"It's useful to her. She learns things."

I left via the same door I'd entered through, closing it behind me. I wouldn't encourage further contact with Lord Darnley. His moods were changeable, and he'd never be someone I could depend on. At first I'd thought that he'd deigned to speak to me because we were both Tudors, but it had only been because he found no threat in my insignificance.

As it turned out, I did matter to Lord Darnley, albeit in a very small way. At the end of January, the queen gave him permission to join his father in Scotland. The night before his departure, right after the queen had retired and I was in my bedroom, my serving woman told me he was at the door of my suite, asking to speak to me. "And he's got a small dog with him," she said, as though amazed. "It looks like a puppy. I can't tell because he's holding it."

I told her to light more candles in the outer room and then wait with her husband in the corridor after showing Lord Darnley in.

"A surprising visit, and at such a late hour," I said when he came in.

He didn't even offer a polite greeting. "You've got to take him," he said directly as he set the puppy down. It ran over to me and bit the hem of my dress.

"Take him?" I asked, confused. I disliked receiving what sounded like the command of a king.

"I'm leaving for Scotland in the morning. I can't take him with me, and I can't leave him with my mother; she'd give him away to anyone who'd take him." There was anger in his tone. "And I won't do that!"

Despite his overbearing manner, he seemed so genuinely upset that I sympathised with him. "What about your brother?" He had a younger one, named Charles. One of the misfortunes of the Countess of Lennox was that out of her eight children, only two sons had survived.

"He's too young. He stays with his tutor in a very small household where there's no room for a dog. And I can't think of anyone else. So, it has to be you. He remembers you, remembers that you liked him. You're no stranger."

"I can't keep him here —"

"But you'll find a good home for him. I'm sure you'll do it."

"You barely know me!"

"I know you're not like everyone else here. You'll do it." Before I could say anything else, he whirled around, threw open the door and left so quickly his cloak rippled out behind him as the door swung shut. Seeing him gone, the puppy let go of my dress, walked to the door and sat down before it, then turned to look back at me. Still startled, I went and picked him up, feeling the smoothness of his coat. He looked up at me with accepting brown eyes, indicating he wasn't disturbed by his changed circumstances.

The servants came back in, staring at me with deep interest. "He's a greyhound," I offered in explanation. "Lord Darnley's going to Scotland and can't take him."

"Do you mean for him to stay here, my lady?" The man sounded as though he hoped the answer would be yes.

But his wife stepped forward and said, "Greyhounds are hunting dogs, my lady. He should be somewhere where he can run and play. A palace is no place for him."

She was right. It was best I found a home for him with at least a garden. And if I did marry and have a child, a dog could be a complication.

"Bring me my cloak," I said, after a moment's thought. "I think I know the perfect place for him."

Less than a quarter of an hour later, I was once again in a surprised Mr. Keyes' parlour as the puppy ran about on the floor.

"My home in Lewisham would be fine," he said agreeably, as soon as I'd told him what I was seeking. "My children would be delighted to have a new puppy there."

"Thank you so very much. I was at a loss as to what to do. Although I would love to have a pet dog, it really would be too much for me to keep him in my suite here, even though I do have two rooms. I thought of the drawing of your lovely house, and how you described it as full of pets. I know so few people to ask, and although we're still new friends, I already know you're someone to be relied on." It occurred to me that, oddly, Lord Darnley had said something similar about me.

"You flatter me," he replied. He was without his coat, wearing a heavy woollen vest over a white shirt above his breeches. In his more informal attire he looked a little more relaxed than usual, as though without his coat he was less aware of his important position as Sergeant Porter. I had a passing thought that I too might seem different when I wasn't wearing the queen's livery.

"Darnley's your second cousin, isn't he?" he asked.

"Yes. But I barely know him beyond polite acknowledgements. I was very surprised when he appeared at my door with the puppy tonight, asking me to take him. It's only because the other day I happened upon him letting the puppy run about for exercise in an empty room. I lingered and played for a little while. They seemed very fond of each other, and this separation must be difficult for them."

"We become more set in our ways as we age. But they're both young. Youth adjusts to change — especially, I'd imagine, if marrying a queen is involved. I'm sure you know everyone thinks that's why Darnley's going to Scotland, despite the idiotic story of our queen wanting Mary Stuart to marry the Earl of Leicester. I even overheard the porters talking about it today."

"Lord Darnley knows it too; he mentioned it when we spoke. Not very agreeably, either. He seemed to be afraid of something dangerous happening to him in Scotland."

Mr. Keyes made a face that suggested he not only understood, but agreed with that possibility. "He should be careful, where that queen is involved. There are lots of stories that she's a slippery one. There was a reason why after the death of her French king husband, she got sent back from

France so quickly. They'd had enough of her. It's not surprising your cousin would prefer to stay here, with his puppy for company."

"But as you said, a crown is an incentive. He's ambitious."

"Then he should make the most of his opportunity," he said knowingly. "When you're older, it's a sorry thing to think you didn't try as much as you might have." His words were wistful, but before I could ask why, he changed the subject. "So, we now have the puppy to care for. He'll be a welcome addition to the household at Lewisham. I'll send word to my son to come fetch him tomorrow. You must promise, though, to visit him there. Perhaps in the spring, when the weather is finer. For now, let's see if we can make him feel at home here — although he seems to have done so already."

As we'd spoken, the puppy had pulled a cushion from a chair and was dragging it around as though it were a playfellow. I went to retrieve it, but Mr. Keyes stopped me, saying it was replaceable if torn apart. Then, he went to the table, where I saw some plates with food on them. "I'm fortunate to have friends in the kitchens who send me gifts sometimes. Tonight, it couldn't have been more useful — a roast chicken. I have half of it left, which my new friend here should devour in no time." He shredded some onto the plate with his fingers, then placed it on the floor. Immediately, the puppy ran over and ate it. Mr. Keyes then went to a cabinet and produced a small bowl, filling it from a pitcher on the table. "Not wine," he said while he did. "I seldom drink it, although it's easier to come by in the palace than good drinking water." He set it on the floor, and the puppy, having finished the chicken, eagerly drank from it.

"It was right for me not to try to keep him," I said. "I know nothing about what dogs eat, or what their care should involve.

I don't think my servants do, either. But you seem to know exactly what to do."

"I've had many, many dogs throughout my life — mastiffs, spaniels, terriers, and others. Never greyhounds, though, so this is a first for me. But it's good, I think, to have something new in one's life. It'll be good for my children too. It can be easy to forget that it's important." He half smiled. "How foolish I must sound! It makes me see how stodgy and fixed I've become to be talking about this as such a change."

"You already knew he'd eat the chicken. I wouldn't have known even that."

"Most of their diet is poultry and bran bread. And game, when available, although it's not too plentiful around the city, even out in Lewisham. For a puppy, some broth and goats' milk is good too."

"Do they live in the house with the family? My parents had so many they had a kennel for them."

"We've always allowed it, but we've never had so many at one time as to need a kennel."

The puppy, having finished his meal, returned to the pillow on the floor. But this time, instead of resuming playing with it, he lay down on top of it and curled up, as though ready to go to sleep.

"It's difficult to imagine him looking more comfortable," I said appreciatively. "Thank you so much for this. And for not minding being disturbed at this late hour."

"It's not so late."

"I'll leave you now to your rest." I felt satisfied that my efforts for the puppy had been so successfully concluded. His future promised to be nicer and much more peaceful than Lord Darnley's did. But then, as Mr. Keyes had said, I couldn't fault my cousin for being ambitious. His feelings about trying to fulfil his rightful place in life must have been as strong as my own. If he and Mary Stuart married and had a son, his claim to the throne would be promoted by the Catholics and might succeed, especially if there was no other as an alternative. In going to Scotland, Lord Darnley was closer to achieving his ambitions than I was. It was time for me to take the next step in advancing my own.

On the table beside the plates was the little wooden box of cards I'd seen during my last visit. I asked, "Can you teach me to play cards? You offered to the last time I was here."

"Yes, I would enjoy doing so very much."

"When would be convenient?"

"Often this is the time when I miss playing them, at the end of the day when my responsibilities are done. I like it best, and I think you might also. Could you try coming at the same time tomorrow?"

"That would be fine. It's rare that the queen needs more than her closest attendants after she retires at night. And my servants would know where to find me, should I be called."

"We can play for an hour or so."

"I look forward to it. Until tomorrow, then. And once again, thank you so much for taking on this little responsibility." We both looked at the cushion, where the puppy was fast asleep.

5

The following evening, I made my way to Mr. Keyes' suite, as arranged.

"There are many different games that are popular now," he said when we sat down across from each other at the table, and he picked up the deck he'd set out. Beside us, the candelabra flickered in the breeze from the window, which was slightly open since the weather had turned surprisingly mild for early February. The room felt more peaceful but emptier than the day before, since the puppy had been sent to Lewisham.

He spread the cards out on the table and slowly explained the rules of one game, which were easy to understand. "Rather simple, isn't it?" I then asked.

"So it may seem," he said, smiling mysteriously. "You'll be surprised at how complicated the games can become. How many variations are possible."

"I imagine there's always luck involved. No matter how skilled one is, there must be."

With a swipe of his hand, he gathered all the cards together and began shuffling them. "Of course. But even more important is intuition, having some kind of sense about how the game is going, and one's chances. When to stay in it, and when to get out. And even whether to participate or not in the first place."

"It must be like other things in life, when sometimes one merely feels it's the right time to do a thing. Maybe circumstances or events point to it, but in the end, it's usually because of a feeling that one decides."

"Yes," he agreed. "But they aren't always right. There have been times when I've been absolutely sure I'd play to win, and went on to lose a sum of money I shouldn't have. And then there have been other times the reverse has happened. Often, though, your feelings are what you can rely on." He stopped shuffling and tucked all the cards into a neat pile, then slid the deck towards the centre of the table. "A good rule I use is that if I don't feel my chances of winning are at least half, I don't play. I can afford to lose some money if I'm wrong, but not very often."

"I'm sorry. I didn't think to bring any cash with me."

He stared at me as though not understanding, but then said quickly, "Oh, no, we're not playing with money. That wouldn't be very fair of me, would it, on your first game? No, no money, not for a while yet. I'll explain wagering to you later — you should know how. I expect that before long, you'll be playing with all those courtiers in the palace with nothing else to do."

"I'm not sure I'd be good enough, and I'm not sure I'd like to. I've seen those games go on for a long, long time. And some of the people playing don't look like they're enjoying themselves very much."

He looked at me seriously. "An important thing to learn is who you can play with, and who you can't. In the palace, you get to know people. There are some who can't stop playing, even when they're losing. They keep thinking that one more game could turn everything around for them after long stretches of losing, and they'll win everything back. Sometimes they do, but rarely. Usually, they end up losing a fortune, and even going into debt. You'll get to know who those people are, and you should avoid them. You don't feel very good after you've won their money. I think it's simply not fair to take it, because something inside those people won't let them stop when they should. I like a nice, even game."

His sentiments were admirable, as so much about him was. With every encounter, I was finding him to be exactly the type of man I'd hoped to find. If my opinion didn't change for the next month or so, I'd make a quiet suggestion about the future. "I'm going to learn this," I said suddenly, with determination. "I might even be able to play with the queen!"

"Maybe so," he replied. "That's the right attitude! And why not? She's your cousin, after all. But you should know, she's very, very good. I've heard she always plays to win."

"I can too," I said. "Let's begin."

For the next month, I had lessons nearly every night for an hour or so, almost entirely without interruption; Mr. Keyes was only called to the Water Gate a couple of times to solve some issue. I'd told my servants I was teaching him Spanish, to help him with his work, which they seemed to believe. The tale was necessary because I'd decided that they may find my cardplaying a little strange, it being so untypical for me. I'd wondered what I'd do to dispel any notions that the visits were romantic in purpose, but my servants gave no indication that they were harbouring such thoughts. It was probably beyond their imagining, based on what they knew of me.

We started out with games for two players, One and Thirty, All Fours, and others, then moved on to those requiring more people, like Primo and Brelan, during which he skilfully pretended to be the other players as well. It was a strange thing for me to be learning, but each night when I arrived back at my own rooms it was with a sense that something was being accomplished, that I was no longer merely drifting along. From time to time, we would chat about other things, too. He told me of his four children at Lewisham, his two sons and two daughters, and his younger brother and sister who lived there with them. It was clear he derived satisfaction from having such a family, and it was only when he mentioned his late wife that there were any hints of sadness. But over the month, they became less frequent, and I began to think that his great grief was easing. He began to seem more interested in what was happening at the palace, and was eager to hear from me all sorts of minor daily news about the queen and her attendants. "I see visitors when they arrive and leave," he told me. "It's nice to finally know something of what happens in between!"

I knew for sure that there'd been more than a passing change in him when at the beginning of March, he told me he'd accepted an invitation to participate in the Shrove Tuesday tournament the following week. The Shrove Tuesday festivities were always some of the liveliest at the palace, since they were followed by Lent, during which the opposite mood would prevail. "I've done it many times in the past," he said. "It's unusual for me to be asked because I'm not a knight, but they've included me because I can ride so well and I'm strong. It takes much effort to unseat me from my horse, and they know it!"

I said I was surprised that they had waited so long to ask him.

"They asked in January when they began to plan it, and I said no. It didn't feel right to do it this year. But a week ago they still needed someone and asked again, and I told them yes. It wouldn't have been very appreciative of me to say no a second time, would it? It's an honour that they include me. And it's good that the nobles and other important folk around here see me as someone beyond the fellow who tends to the gates and holds the peace. I've been thinking that there may be more for me in life. Sergeant Porter and Captain of Sandgate Castle have been fine, but there may be more to seek."

I was glad to hear this expression of ambition. "Do you have enough time to prepare?"

"I've already sent to Lewisham for the knight's costume armour I've worn in other years. It's a little silly, intentionally old-fashioned, but these tournaments are for show. You must tell me afterwards how you think I look in it."

"I'm sure you'll make a fine knight." Indeed, he might become one permanently, if things went the way I wanted. "You must be careful. I know the jousting is only pretend, but you must take care."

"It's more in the riding. I'll go down and practise beforehand, with the others."

We decided that while he was preparing, our cardplaying would stop. I was already proficient — the games had been easy for me to learn, and he'd repeatedly complimented me on my skill — so it seemed both of us tacitly understood that when we resumed the visits, it would be because we liked each other's company. It would be time then to ask him whether he could consider a marriage between us. Although I was unsure of what his answer would be, I was certain that a refusal wouldn't create any difficulty for me, for I was confident he would speak of it to no one.

The tournament was as spectacular as expected, with elaborate details based mostly on the legends of King Arthur and his Knights of the Round Table. When I saw from the stands that day that the participating lords and gentlemen were some of the most important courtiers, I understood Mr. Keyes' inclusion hadn't only been because of his strength and riding ability. He was liked and respected by all involved, and regarded as their equal. Contrary to what he'd told me, his costume armour didn't look foolish or silly, but impressive, as did his being the largest participant. That he was older than nearly any other gentleman was unnoticeable, and he rode his horse with more dexterity and ease than most of them. The queen applauded him as generously as she did anyone else, which I saw with satisfaction from where I sat further back behind her.

The Countess of Lennox, sitting beside her, applauded him also, although a second later, as though following her lead. The queen had continued to single her out for small honours since Lord Darnley had left for Scotland, and the countess, keenly alert at all times, was clearly intent on keeping her position. There had been much talk among the courtiers of her son's reception in Scotland. Mary Stuart had been gracious to him, and he'd made an excellent impression everywhere. There hadn't, though, been any discussion of marriage. It was said that the important Scottish earls, being mostly Reformed, would oppose it because of the strongly Catholic ties of the Lennox family. But other stories had drifted down from Holyrood and the other Scottish palaces that Queen Mary and Lord Darnley were often together. Yet if any of this news, which had undoubtably reached Queen Elizabeth, had disturbed her, she didn't show it. Whatever her own schemes or intentions were regarding having allowed Lord Darnley to go to Scotland, nothing had as yet displeased her. From all appearances, she remained in complete accord with the Countess of Lennox.

At the supper in the queen's apartments following the tournament, the countess was once again seated next to her, while I was much further away, nearly out of the large room used for such occasions. This was often so, especially when the courtiers were intended to be on display as an extension of the queen's beauty and splendour. The countess was still a handsome woman; she looked the way one would expect a member of the royal family to look. For me, the opposite was true. Although it was never stated outright, it was understood by the stewards and organising officials — and by me — that because of my condition, I was to be placed as inconspicuously as possible. It was something I'd never objected to or disliked, since I usually would have preferred not to be in attendance at all. Much more unpleasant had been the few times when the queen had brought me forward in an attentive way, which I'd understood had been to make a silent political statement to whoever was with her about my unsuitability as a successor.

Mr. Keyes sat importantly with the gentlemen from the tournament in places of honour close to the queen. Like the others, he'd changed out of his knight's costume, and now wore a tan doublet with sections of intricate brown and white patterning. It was a garment that would have obscured within it any of the other gentlemen, but because of his size, it looked fine on him. From where I sat so far away across the room, I thought that if fortune gifted me a child who resembled him, it would always be seated beside the queen, or perhaps eventually even in her place.

Several times throughout the supper he looked towards me, smiling, the only one in the crowded room who acknowledged my presence. A number of the other gentlemen sat with their wives, and I found myself wondering how it would feel to be sitting beside him. Quickly, I pushed the thought away. If a marriage came to pass between us, it would have to remain unknown for many, many months, if not longer, until any child we'd conceived was about to be born. Undoubtedly, it would take time for the queen to reconcile herself to such a development. But so long as I gave birth to child whose parents had without question been appropriately married, it wouldn't matter. There would be a new heir to the throne who would eventually have to be acknowledged. With that in mind, being able to sit together at a table with Mr. Keyes as my husband seemed a very minor thing indeed.

There was to be dancing in the next room, and as supper concluded the musicians could already be heard playing there. The queen would no doubt be partnered by Robert Dudley, who'd participated in the tournament in a very prominent way, and sat at supper on the other side of her from the Countess of Lennox as though he thought no place could be more fitting for him. It was speculated that he still hoped to marry her, although she seemed increasingly disinclined to marry him, or anyone. The queen had let it be known that her recently making him Earl of Leicester had been to increase his appeal to Mary Stuart as a husband, and it was believed that if successful, Mary's formal recognition as the future successor to the English throne would follow it. Lord Robert, though, had from the first shown a complete disinterest in the marriage, and made no effort to journey to Scotland to further the matter in person. There were several rumours as to why, one being that he believed it was a test of his devotion to Queen Elizabeth, and another that he was deterred by the dangerous reputation of the Scottish queen. The latter drew smiles from those who repeated it, for Lord Robert had such a reputation himself. But no matter the reason, he had remained in England while Lord Darnley had been sent to Scotland, and he stayed much beside the queen, as he did today. When the supper was over, and the finger bowls had been presented, used, and taken away, he stood with everyone else when the queen did, and, extending his wrist for her to place her hand upon, led her into the other room to dance.

Amid much convivial chatter, partly the result of the large amounts of wine that had been consumed during the supper, everyone began crowding together to follow them in. I held back, intending to quietly slip away. Although I'd been taught dancing as part of my education, and had shown ability, my condition had halted it, and I doubted that by now I'd remember what to do. Mrs. Parry, knowing it wasn't for me, had at the start of the supper kindly told me it wasn't necessary for me to remain, and I would now leave as soon as the room cleared.

Mr. Keyes found me while I was waiting. He said, "Some of the others who aren't dancing are going to play cards. There'll be several games. Since you've become so competent at them, I thought you might like to join one. We could find two others for a game of four."

He'd mentioned my doing so before, but I was quite taken aback by the thought of it actually happening. For an instant, it was appealing, especially if the queen were to see me doing so. But I knew that for what I hoped to achieve, I shouldn't at present be seen with him more than briefly. Very soon, he might understand why. "No, thank you," I replied. "I should retire now. But you go ahead, and I wish you good luck. Tomorrow, can we resume our own games?"

"Yes! Why wouldn't we?"

"It being Ash Wednesday, I didn't know whether you'd want to. Or even at all, during the Lent season."

"I don't believe God would disapprove," he said with respectful dismissiveness. "If we follow the Lent dietary curtailments, surely that's satisfactory for him. Until tomorrow, then. And with the good luck you've wished me, I'm sure I'm going to win tonight." He bowed and went back to the crowd making their way to the other room.

There were just a few lingering courtiers about to go into the other room to dance when I started moving towards the other door to the corridor. I was nearly there when I thought I heard my name being spoken behind me. Turning, I saw Lord Henry Seymour coming towards me. At once, I checked to see who else was still in the room, for my being observed in conversation with the brother of the man my sister had married — or hadn't, as the queen insisted — would be unwise. But at that same moment the last of the other courtiers left, the music became louder, signalling that the queen had taken to the dance floor, and all the servers clearing the tables stopped and rushed to the door to watch. The time was right, and I waited, eager to hear what he had to tell me of Catherine and her children. I followed him to a side window seat, somewhat secluded, where we sat.

I could see he would have preferred not to have the conversation, but he was the type who felt he should because of loyalty to his family. It should have been a carefree, enjoyable day for him, participating in the tournament and festivities. I never liked being at such events, but he would have, especially having been so recently included. "This can wait," I told him, "if you'd rather be in there with the others."

"I wouldn't," he answered simply, though he was looking towards the door everyone else had gone through.

The following evening, when we sat down to play cards, I told Mr. Keyes of the encounter. "Henry Seymour spoke to me yesterday — after the supper when the room was empty, which we made sure of," I said. "He's as careful as I am. Even though he wasn't involved in his brother's marriage plans, the queen wasn't quick to have him back here at the palace, and he wants to stay."

"Harry's a fine young fellow," he replied. "He rode with skill yesterday, and everyone liked him."

"I'd wondered if his being included was a sign of improvement in the queen's attitude toward his brother and my sister. I'd thought it also when he first became a courtier again a few weeks ago. I couldn't ask about it, of course. I can't do anything that might make it seem like I'm becoming involved in my sister's situation."

"But you're concerned about her."

"How couldn't I be? But I have to be as careful as Lord Henry. I appreciated the news he gave me, although it wasn't what I would have hoped for. There's been no change in the queen's feelings about Catherine. Lord Henry believes he was allowed back because his mother is still a powerful figure for the Reformers, and the queen wants to show she respects her, despite the behaviour of her other son. Yet it shouldn't be seen as anything more than that."

"Not surprising," Mr. Keyes said, shuffling the cards slowly. "The queen can't alienate the Reformers."

"She might have this morning, at the Ash Wednesday sermon outside Westminster Abbey. You weren't there, were you? I looked for you but didn't see you."

"No, I wasn't. I would have gone; I like being a part of the crowds that come whenever a sermon's given in a courtyard. It's intended to draw them, even though I'm sure many are only there to see the queen. But today I was busy downstairs at the gate. So, what happened?"

"When the preacher began to talk badly of a new book written by a Catholic that praised the old use of pictures and statues in church, the queen called out for him to stop. He must not have heard her at first, for he continued. But he stopped when she repeated her order, telling him further that the subject was already known to all. He finished his sermon differently, and quickly, but the queen looked displeased when she left. I'm sure those courtiers who still believe in the Catholic ways are going to make much of it, seeing it as a sign she's beginning to lean toward them — especially since she's had important Catholics around her lately, like the Countess of Lennox. And people are thinking about why an eligible Lord Darnley was allowed to go to Scotland, with Mary Stuart seeking a new husband. If they marry, a Catholic claim to the English succession would be stronger, although consolidated. People are aware of that, and the queen knows they are. So, she tries to keep everyone wondering who she really likes, a Catholic today, a Reformer tomorrow."

"She's a masterful politician. She plays her political games with great skill."

"For Catherine it's not a game. Lord Henry said they don't often get news of her, and then only indirectly, usually through servants. But they've heard she's increasingly despondent, unable to accept her circumstances."

His face showed he knew there was nothing he or I could do about it. "But she's maintained in comfort in the best of surroundings, isn't she? And isn't her younger son with her?" He placed the cards back on the table between us.

"It's not enough for her. For someone else, maybe, but not her. She wants to be with her husband. Lord Henry said she wrote another letter to the queen, who wouldn't even respond to it. So, she remains where she is, with no chance of the queen changing her mind." With the surrounding empty table, the little deck of cards looked suddenly alone. "Someone else might prosper in solitude, someone given to study and learning. Even if they weren't that way naturally, they might learn to be different. But that's not Catherine."

"It can't be easy for you to see what's become of her."

"It isn't. I feel sorry for her, but at the same time I can't approve of her short-sightedness and carelessness. She has two sons, either of whom could have become the next king. But from what I know of the queen, that's not going to happen, ever. She'll always think Catherine got around how she wanted things done, and she's showing that she can undo it. By refusing to acknowledge the marriage, she's found a way to demonstrate she can't be outwitted. And she's making sure everyone else sees it. It's not only Catherine, either. The Earl of Hertford has done everything wrong as well, both in the beginning and lately. Surely, he knew of the attempt last year to have European scholars help validate the marriage, and he should've stopped it. Anyone who knows the queen should have known it would never succeed with her. Now, she'll never change her mind."

"Other opinions in this country matter as well," Mr. Keyes suggested, helpfully. "The queen knows Parliament's important, even if she doesn't have to do what they want. She can't always ignore them, especially about an issue like this. And there's always what the common folk want."

"But there's something beyond the queen's personal feelings that's even more significant. Something I'm sure she understands. No one's going to want a king whose right to the throne could be questioned. For my sister's sons, it always can be. It could be manipulated by either the Catholics or Reformers for their own purposes. And they do manipulate religion, you know. Both sides do it often, when it suits them. There are good people sincere in their beliefs, but there are others who use religion to further their own worldly plans."

We'd never discussed religion at length, but he now said at once, "There are. Everyone knows it. It's not so difficult to work out who they are, either, although many of them don't know what they're really doing. Often, they convince themselves it's for one reason, when it's something else."

It was another of those times when he showed his depth of thought. "It's the world we have," I agreed. "And unfortunately, it shows no sign of changing anytime soon. The queen is right in wanting a stable future for the country. Catherine was irresponsible in not going about what she did in a way that would have provided certainty. She was in a position to provide an heir to the throne. It's not that I resent her trying. It's that she was so careless in how she went about it." I hesitated, thinking it was my last chance not to step into what I was setting before me. On the table, the deck of cards sat as though waiting. But my decision had already been made a while ago. "I'd have done it very differently. And I still would, if I ever try to."

"Try to...?" he asked slowly, but as though he was already starting to understand what the answer would be.

"To have a child."

"I didn't know marriage was in your future plans," he then said in a surprised tone.

"It is. Especially now that it's clear Catherine's children won't succeed the queen. I feel I have a responsibility to fulfil in having one. But I suppose you're wondering, given the way I look, if I'm able to."

He started to say no, but I stopped him, with a slight wave of my hand. "Please, don't feel that way. It's an expected question — one that I had myself. So, in January I consulted one of the best doctors in the country to get the answer. It was yes. But because of my condition I might not be able to later, for it's almost certain to become more pronounced as I age, and that would diminish the chances. If I want to have a child, I shouldn't wait."

"Would the queen let you marry?" He was looking at me with interest. It was a good sign that he hadn't immediately sought to withdraw from the topic.

"No. Almost certainly, she would not. Since I can't take a chance on her refusing, I'd have to marry without her knowledge, like my sister did. But it would absolutely have to be done in a way so that Catherine's mistakes were avoided. And the queen shouldn't know until a child was on its way — a child who might one day become king or queen."

A long moment passed in silence. Then, he said, "Yes. I can see that could happen, if it was done in the right way."

"It would have to be. First would be making sure my choice of husband was right. The doctor spoke to me about what type of man would be best to increase the possibility of my child's stature not repeating my own. By myself, I've thought through the other qualities he should have. It would have to be someone reliable, of excellent character, and who's not political. Someone who won't make it seem like either the Catholics or the Reformers are involved, and whose child might then be acceptable to both sides." I took a deep breath. "Someone like you."

He moved suddenly, placing both his hands flat on the table. "What a thing to say about me," he then said quietly, as though in disbelief.

"Why? You'd be the perfect choice."

His eyes widened in astonishment. Having said as much as I already had, I felt it was best for me to be direct. I asked, "Is remarrying something you've thought of?"

"Yes, and no. But never a marriage like this."

"Would you consider it?" I leaned forward a little and spoke quickly. "I know I don't look the ideal choice for a wife, but, like I said, I'm capable of having a child. I've already been clear with you about why I want to. I don't deny or minimise the problems that could occur, the possible consequences for us. The queen's anger isn't to be lightly disregarded. But politically, her success has come from the fact that she looks ahead. There's a good chance she might see the benefit of having another option for a successor. At the least, she wouldn't be able to deny the soundness of the claim. It's even possible that she could decide the future would be easier if she approved it. And if she does, it would make you the father of the next king or queen."

He suddenly pushed his chair back, then stood and went to the window. But instead of looking out, he turned around. "There are other claims to the throne," he said quietly.

"Mine is the best. I stand in the succession right after my sister. My cousin Margaret, the Lady Strange, comes after me. The Queen of Scotland and the Countess of Lennox aren't in it at all. Any other claim is distant."

"I'm not even a knight."

"You already have everything to merit becoming one. Even if you didn't, it wouldn't matter. Things are changing in this country. The aristocracy is less important and the new men more so. The queen has many around her in important positions who are new men whose success has been because of their own talents. A future king or queen who drew from both sides would be appreciated."

Even from across the room I could see his expression change to one of fascination, as though a vision of a future he'd never imagined for himself suddenly danced before him. Then he turned around, threw open the window, and half leaned out, breathing in the air of the Thames so deeply I could hear it. As he did, a gust of wind blew in past him, causing the candelabra to flicker but not go out as it continued to provide the only light in the room.

"The candles?" he asked, turning around as he drew the window shut.

"They're all fine."

"An omen, perhaps?"

"They're not things I believe in. I believe in myself. The future depends on what I do."

He slowly came back and sat down in his chair again, but without pulling it close to the table. "Yes, I can see that."

"Don't misunderstand me; I do believe in things. I listen to the sermons and find meaning in some of them. I've read the Bible and I think about some of its passages. When the wind came in a minute ago, I thought of the light shining in the darkness, refusing to be overcome."

"We need to continue our conversation," he said. "Our unexpected, but very interesting conversation."

So far, his response had been everything I'd hoped for. But I knew he would need time to make a decision, and be sure of it. I said, "I didn't speak to you of this lightly, or on a whim. It's been on my mind since January, when you and I first crossed paths. It was right after I'd decided to move forward with this, and it did feel like you appeared when I was ready for you to be there. But I'm not the type of person who uses other people. I had to get to know you, to see if it might be something that could benefit your life as much as my own. I've decided it is. But I'm not a fool, and I understand what I'm asking. You must be certain." I leaned back in my chair and folded my hands before me. "And so, Mr. Keyes, I think it best that we not see each other for some time while you think this over. You must think deeply and consider every aspect. After that, we can continue our conversation."

"Yes," he replied distantly. "I should think."

"Perhaps I should return in a week? We might not be ready to make a decision by then, but at least it won't be so new to you."

"I won't need that long. A day or so, at most."

He seemed to be about to say more, but I said at once, "No, I insist. Anything less wouldn't be fair to you. I've had months to consider it. A week, at least."

"What an ingrate I would be not to have an answer by then. Lady Mary, you can expect it."

"Very good. I'm sure you know this isn't something to be spoken of to anyone else. Eventually, yes, but even then, only to those we need to ensure the marriage is valid. It's best that as few people as possible know of it. That is, assuming we decide to move forward."

"Assuming we do." Still sitting, he pulled his chair forward and picked up the deck of cards that had remained unused on the table. "We have time for One and Thirty before you leave," he said, smiling at me in a very confident way that left me in little doubt as to what his answer would be a week from now.

6

During the days that followed we saw each other at dinner and supper, and I took it as a good sign that he made no effort to avoid our eyes sometimes meeting, which was often. I began to think what our next steps should be, after we'd agreed to take them. Some were obvious decisions, such as observing the custom of waiting to marry until Lent was over. But there were other matters on which I would need to hear his opinions. It was absolutely necessary that we be equal partners; children, I had seen, did best in stable families, becoming adults who were ready for complicated and important positions in life, and there was none more so than that of a king or queen.

There was news that week from Scotland, talked of quietly but with interest among the courtiers: unbeknown to almost everyone, Queen Elizabeth had instructed her ambassador to tell Queen Mary that she had no intention of declaring a successor until she had herself fully decided that marriage was not for her. Even should Mary marry the Earl of Leicester, there would still be no commitment, and there was no mention of Lord Darnley at all. Queen Mary, it was said, had wept and secluded herself in her rooms after ordering the ambassador from the palace.

Most of the courtiers believed that Lord Darnley and his father would soon be recalled from Scotland, as it seemed the queen's decision would apply to him as much as to the Earl of Leicester. But there was no news of it, and the Countess of Lennox continued as the queen's daily companion. I wondered if anyone besides me surmised that the queen was slyly pushing Mary to attempt to strengthen her claim to the English throne by marrying Lord Darnley without her approval, which would provide Elizabeth with a reason to refuse to acknowledge the succession claims of both. Meanwhile, the countess was undoubtedly trying her best to subtly convince the queen of the benefits the marriage could bring her, placing her reasons as skilfully as chess pieces. It now being Lent — during which it was unlikely a marriage, approved or not, would take place — provided a stretch of time for both to consider their strategies more deeply. After Easter, bolder and more decisive moves would be expected, and at that time, the marriage of Mr. Keyes and myself would enter us into the game also. But we would try our best to ensure neither the queen, nor the countess, nor anyone else knew about it for as long as possible.

Mr. Keyes' response during our last conversation had left me almost certain of what he would tell me when we met again, and it was with confidence that I entered his apartment when I returned. But I was surprised when instead of leading me to the parlour as usual, he said he wanted to show me the roof deck, the stairway to which I'd once seen in the room furthest out over the river.

He was wearing his coat and holding a small blanket, folded in half. "Your shawl won't be sufficient outside, so this can serve as a second one," he said, reaching behind me and starting to drape it around the one I always wore during winter while making my way through the palace corridors. Involuntarily, I started to pull away, the way I'd learned to after arriving at the palace and finding there were people who believed touching a hunchback would bring them good luck. But I instantly stopped, not wanting him to misunderstand and think I found his touch unpleasant or his courtesy unappreciated. I gestured for him to continue, which he did, very carefully. "I'm sorry I jumped a little," I said hesitantly, for it was something I'd never spoken of to anyone, not even Mrs. Parry after she'd seen it happen and then reluctantly explained to me why. "Oftener than you might think, there are those who believe that touching a hunchback brings them good luck."

With contempt, Mr. Keyes replied, "I don't know which is worse, their cruelty or their stupidity."

"They're fools to believe it. Even if it mattered, I'm not the hunchback they think me; my condition is different. If I bring anyone luck, it's for other reasons."

"I already count myself lucky for you to have befriended me," he assured me. He looked down at me kindly. "You'd better pull the blanket up over your head and bonnet. It's usually windy on the deck, and tonight should be no exception."

I arranged it hood-like, and then followed him to the room with the stairs, where he placed the metal candle-lantern he'd been carrying on the centre table. "It would likely go out at once outside, so I'm leaving it here. The moon is almost full and the night is clear, so we won't need it." Approaching the stairs, he told me to hold the rail.

At the top of the narrow staircase was a door which he pushed open on its hinges, then closed again after we were both on the deck, which looked wider than I'd imagined it would. The latticework around the edges was tall but did not diminish the sense of openness. The night was cloudless, like he'd said it would be, the moon a nearly perfect white orb surrounded by stars as far as the eye could see. Standing beneath such vastness, I felt even smaller and more insignificant than I usually did, and for the first time, Mr. Keyes did not look so large. I suddenly felt that we existed in a place of boundless potential.

"We can speak as privately here as in my rooms," said Mr. Keyes. "You can see there are no windows where the deck meets the wall or nearby, and none overlooking us. Only rarely does anyone come up here at all. It's a strange place; I'm not sure what it was intended for. There are some larger openings in the latticework to see through, but they couldn't be used for defence if the palace needed it. Perhaps they're there to give the best river views, so lookouts can report the first sign of any approaching boat."

I went to one of the openings and looked through. I could see the river in the moonlight, with a few boats with lanterns travelling down it. But the landscape of the shore opposite had only a few points of light showing, as though the soft blanket of sleep had settled over it. Further down the river, around its bend in the most populated part of the city, it would be different, but it couldn't be seen from where we were.

"For all the beauty of the stars, this is still a lonely place," I said.

"Yes. It's only since my wife died that I started coming here occasionally — especially on clear nights, for the stars give me comfort I couldn't find elsewhere."

"At least you found something to help."

"Many never do. I was fortunate — even more so when you became part of my life, although it wasn't until you asked if I might marry you that I understood it. Only then did it occur to me that I hadn't visited this place for a while. And, that I no longer felt so lonely and without purpose. That's because of you."

I'd known he liked my companionship, but not that he was so grateful for it. "Thank you," I answered, although so brief a reply felt completely inadequate compared to the sincerity and depth of what he'd said.

It was windy on the deck, but not as much as he'd expected. I threw the blanket off my bonnet and breathed in deeply. Appearing to be in thought, he took a few steps away, but then turned back to me. "In the last month of her life, my wife said something that led me to believe she thought ambition absent in me, especially for the future of our children. It was the first time she ever said so. The idea may have been new to her, perhaps the result of her illness or knowledge of her nearing absence from our lives. I don't know what prompted it, but now that she's gone it's lingered in my mind. At my age, unaccomplished ambitions usually remain so. Until, that is, you spoke to me last week, and I saw how your ambition could partner with my own. No matter what she thought, my wife would want me to take the opportunity for our sons and daughters to become half-siblings of a child who could follow the queen on the throne."

I went to him and held the sleeve of his coat. "Isn't it our right to try? What are we if we don't?"

He placed his hand on top of mine. "We should marry after Easter, in April. Are we in agreement?"

"It's what I've hoped for almost since we first met! But I had to be sure." Our hands clasped, seeming to finalise it. "You accept wherever this course leads us, whether we succeed or not?"

"Yes!" He said it without hesitation. "We must try."

"There's likely to be difficulty with the queen when she first finds out. I believe, though, she'll resign herself to it, once she understands there are no political motives or allies behind it. She may even see it as advantageous for her to have another option for a successor, one that could balance whatever is happening with my other relatives. But it would be best for a child to be on its way before she knows anything. Ideally, to have been already born. And to be a boy."

"A future king," he said, as though still amazed at the thought of it.

"Or a queen, if a girl. Either would occupy the same place in the succession. Although there would be more security from possible challengers if the child were a boy. Mary Stuart is surely going to have children with her next husband, whether Lord Darnley or someone else. And Lord Darnley should as well. So, we must be absolutely meticulous in avoiding anything that could cause our marriage to be questioned. There's no room for error, none at all. Our child's claim to the throne must be the best it can be."

The wind had stopped, and in the moonlight the empty deck looked calm and still. But it was no longer a time for stillness for us. Mr. Keyes wanted to show me the place because it held meaning for him, but we now had to leave it and make our future plans. I suggested we go back inside, and he agreed.

In the parlour he took the still lit candle from the lantern and touched it to each of those in the candelabra while I removed my blanket-cloak and carefully folded it. He then took it and went into the other room, returning without his coat, but holding a small cloth bag made of velvet and tied with a ribbon. "These are for you," he said as he withdrew three rings, one by one, and then a small scent bottle with a gold chain of the type women wore attached to their belt on their side. First, he gave me the bottle, which was made of mother of pearl. "I'll look quite the fashionable lady, wearing this," I said gratefully, although I wasn't sure I'd be confident enough to do so.

"Two rings, one gold and one silver, both with little diamonds all around. Hopefully they'll fit. They're meant to be worn together. I had to estimate the size when I bought them."

I took them and slid them onto my right ring finger, where they fit as though I'd chosen them myself. Before I could comment, he picked up the third ring, which was more ornate, a ruby surrounded by four diamonds. "This, is your engagement ring. Wear it with the certainty of my intent. Your left ring finger, please, Lady Mary." I offered my hand, and he slid it into place. Once again, the fit was perfect. I stared at its beauty as it glittered in the candelabra light like the herald of all of our successes that would follow.

Looking at him, I saw he was anxiously waiting for my response. "The ring is lovely," I said. "All of them are, and the bottle, especially for being unexpected."

"Why wouldn't you have an engagement ring? I bought it the day after your last visit. I knew immediately what I wanted to do. I waited a week before telling you because you insisted. But I already knew, and went for the ring at once. I was sure I'd be able to choose the right size, after so many weeks of watching the cards moved about by your fingers. The difficulty was that at the jewellers there were so many beautiful pieces I couldn't leave with merely the engagement ring. I felt you deserved everything I saw. I could have afforded it, all of it — I've wealth enough. But I knew you wouldn't like it if I gave you anything more than a few things. A cabinet full of treasures all at once would be meaningless for you. Over time, one by one, I'll buy you other gifts. That way, I think you'll accept them."

"Nothing else is needed," I answered quietly. I usually went ringless, and on my fingers the beautiful new jewels looked strange. "Although I doubt that I'll be able to dissuade you, you must expect I might try. Meanwhile, you mustn't be offended by my asking that you buy nothing more for me for some time. And I can't wear these now except when I come here. Our plans have to remain between us and as few others as possible, especially here at the palace, for many months ahead."

"I understand. But I do hope you'll wear at least the rings when you're here." His manner changed, becoming more focused and efficient, as though he was about to attend to his work. "We have some very practical things to discuss now. Perhaps we should sit?"

We took our usual seats, but this time the cards remained unused on the table. "So," he began, "it's a month until Easter will have passed, and we have a little time. I'll seek a clergyman to perform the ceremony for us. Have you a preference for one?"

"No, so long as he performs the ceremony according to the Book of Common Prayer."

"I'll be attended by my brother, and perhaps my son also. And one or two others, who I haven't decided yet. Can you provide at least one? A woman would be best."

"No one comes to mind right now. But I'm sure I can find her over the next month. I'll have to make sure it's someone who won't speak of it to anyone else. I understand as thoroughly as you do that the presence of others is essential. The main reason my sister's marriage was set aside was because that hadn't been seen to properly by her or the earl. Their error, I think, was in attempting to minimise the chances of it being talked about afterward by anyone. But then Lady Jane Seymour died and the clergyman vanished."

He hesitated before asking, "You know there were whispers of murder around the palace?"

Lord Darnley had mentioned he thought so as well. "Yes. No one knows if it was or not. But there were important people who didn't want there to be so clear an heir to the throne. Needless to say, we need to be very, very careful ourselves. There'll always be those whose ambition is personal and not political, but we do have the advantage of not being so prominently linked to the Reformed faction. There's every chance of our child being acceptable to both sides."

"You're confident, aren't you?" He smiled agreeably.

"We said before, we have to try."

"The final thing I wanted to mention is that I think we should each write a letter to the other, with our intentions of marrying clearly stated in them. Before the ceremony, they should be dated and sealed and given to others for safekeeping. An important part of a marriage is to show that the bride and groom stated their intent beforehand. If needed, the letters can be shown. Although I'm hoping they'll remain unnecessary."

"Now, Mr. Keyes, the confidence is on your part. But I completely agree about the letters. It seems we are very much of the same mind."

"It's time for you to use my given name: Thomas. Only when we are here, of course, for the time being."

"And you must call me Mary." And it was with that simplicity that so important a change between us was signified.

We then spoke of other related matters, including how he intended to have his children visit during the next month so he could introduce me, without explaining why. It was then that I thought to ask him about the puppy I'd got from Lord Darnley, and given to him.

"He's quite settled and content in his new home," he answered, "and a favourite of everyone there already. Being so young, he's never seen a spring yet, only winter. No doubt he's going to thoroughly enjoy the new world on the gardens and grounds he'll begin to discover in a month or so. When you meet my children, you must ask about him."

On my way back to my rooms, I thought about the puppy again and the fortuitous change in his life. I wondered if Lord Darnley was as comfortable in the new Scottish surroundings he found himself in — or rather, those that his parents, the queen, and politics had placed him in.

7

The next morning everyone was surprised when the Countess of Lennox and a boy who looked to be about seven years old entered the queen's outer room. From his fair hair and resemblance to Lord Darnley, it was obvious he was his younger brother Charles, who'd been spoken of at court but had never yet made an appearance. The countess, not serving in the rotation of the queen's women that week, was not dressed in her livery. Instead she was wearing a handsome dress of dark red velvet with sober brown satin sleeves and trim. Above her starkly white ruff her face looked like that of an ancient Roman matron, still powerful and vital despite her advancing years. Any grey in her neatly parted hair was concealed by its blondeness, and her plain brown French bonnet, despite its simplicity, somehow had the look of a crown.

Her son was dressed as any wealthy child would be on such an important occasion, in an outfit of black and brown velvet. He walked with perfect poise, wearing with ease his small white ruff and square plumed hat. Side by side they made a striking impression, one of familial continuity, which doubtless was exactly what the countess wanted for the first time Charles was presented to the queen and all the courtiers. He was a visible reminder that she had not only one son but two who were Tudors, and available to inherit the throne.

Behind them came a stout elderly man, wearing the typical nondescript dark coat and hat of a tutor. As the doors to the inner room opened, the countess turned around slightly and gestured with a finger that he was to remain, which he did as they passed through and the doors swung closed behind them. He then appeared uncomfortable in the crowded room, even though everyone had resumed their own conversations as soon as the countess and Charles were out of sight. Alone, he was of no interest to the courtiers, little more than another of the many servants flowing through their lives. Sadly, I too had often regarded my own servants in such a diminishing way. But in recent months, strangely, there had been small moments when they had started to seem different to me, more like individuals with meaningful lives of their own. Even so, it wasn't only kindness in wanting to alleviate his awkwardness, but the desire for information, that prompted me to go and lead him to a seat off to one side, the type I usually sought for myself.

He thanked me, bowed, and sat down, after I settled in the chair beside. I felt none of the discomfort I usually did when meeting someone new, for he hadn't seemed to notice my condition at all. People of learning, I'd noticed, often didn't, likely because their attention was on intellectual matters rather than physical ones. When I asked if he was Charles's tutor, he replied that he was. I then told him my name.

Immediately, he stared at me, politely but with interest. "May I ask if you are sister to the Jane Grey who was queen so briefly?"

It was a question that came often in similar circumstances. "Jane was my eldest sister. Then came Catherine, and then me. Both my sisters were unfortunate in their choices, although they were very different ones, for different reasons." Carefully, I added, "I'm fortunate in the favour the queen has shown by having me here in her household."

Very quickly, his head turned from me as he scanned the room. The man was no fool, and was checking we weren't being overheard. Then he looked back at me and smiled. "Jane Grey was a great scholar, much admired both here and on the Continent."

This, too, I'd expected; most tutors, especially to the children of the nobility, had heard of her accomplishments. "She was. But I haven't been blessed with those same gifts of intellect."

Of course, it was impossible to discuss learning without touching on the Christian conflict, which he now did. "Hers were respected by both Catholic and Reformed people of learning. The wisest among us understand the importance of studying both sides of these Christian issues, no matter what belief is personally subscribed to. Our queen was educated so, and the Countess of Lennox's son is now being taught the same way, despite how their family is always hailed as possible champions of the Catholics. Indeed, the countess had me make sure Charles was adequately prepared on the subject before coming here today, and that he'd be able to answer with moderation any questions he might be asked on religion. This meeting is especially important, since it was requested by the queen."

"My cousin the countess has enjoyed much of the queen's company of late," I said, a little evasively, and conclusively, for I'd already learned what I'd wanted to know: first, that young Charles was being taught in a way that could render him acceptable politically to both Catholics and Reformers, and secondly, that his appearance at court had been requested by the queen. The request meant she was now beginning to assess the strengths and weaknesses of another player who would shortly enter the game of succession. The countess, having placed one game piece advantageously in Scotland, was ready to start moving another. Soon, though, if I had a child of my own — one with ties to the great scholar Lady Jane Grey, who'd impressed Reformers and Catholics alike — the game might change in ways presently unknown to all. More than ever, I was sure my plan to marry Thomas was the right one, and shouldn't be delayed any longer than necessary. Although I could never look as impressive as the countess had as she'd just passed through the room, attracting the respectful gazes of all, I should still be able to have child with a better claim to the throne than either of hers. And I was becoming increasingly confident that I could outwit both her and the queen in how I did so.

I didn't want to rudely leave the tutor, so I sought to talk a bit further, and asked if there'd been news of how Lord Darnley fared in Scotland.

"Yes, and good enough, I suppose," he answered. "But we've heard nothing regarding if he'll marry the Scots queen. Most people expect that he's going to, but I don't know his own thoughts on that. His tutor was a Scotsman, and I don't know how he was educated. So, it's hard to tell how things might be going for him now, or predict any outcome. It's an unstable situation in Scotland. Much of the country is Reformed, in a stricter way than here, and it's pressed all the time by their chief minister John Knox. But Mary Stuart is Catholic, and it's said she's very much a Frenchwoman in how she thinks and behaves. She's been in conflict with Knox since her return there. So that's the setting our good Lord Darnley has entered. His tutor was Catholic, so it's to be expected that he would be of that faith, especially given the way his parents are viewed as leaders among the Catholics. But I've been told that in practice, he is unpredictable, in religion as well as many other things." He leaned back in his chair and folded his hands together, looking very satisfied to have given so thorough an answer to my simple question. But as I politely excused myself and went out into the corridor, I was thinking not only that the politics of Scotland wouldn't be easy for Lord Darnley to navigate, but that it had been a deliberate move for the queen to have kept his shrewdly talented mother in England when he went.

I was careful not to let my servants see the gifts Thomas had given me, and locked them in the wooden box I kept in my bedroom cabinet for my few valuables. But in the following days when I visited him, I found he liked seeing me wearing the engagement ring. When we played cards, he would look for it, so I started bringing it in my pocket and putting it on before arriving at his door. On my afternoon detours there, I'd do so after I'd visited the wine cellar or kitchen, but sometimes before. Near the end of March, it was noticed by someone when we were both in the kitchen.

I'd known the middle-aged widow Mrs. Goldwell from the few years before I'd come to court, when she'd attended my mother. Not long after my arrival, she'd approached me, seeking a position, and I'd found one for her with the wife of an official in the palace. Occasionally we crossed paths when the court was at Whitehall, and she continually expressed gratitude for my having helped her, despite my assurances that she didn't need to. She'd served my mother well for several years, and it had been the least I could do to assist her.

Although she was tall, with a nicely featured face, there was a quietness about her that often left her unnoticed as she went about her daily tasks. But she was entirely capable of asserting herself, which I'd discovered once while walking beside her in a palace corridor, when we'd heard a loud whisper of "Crouchback Mary" from a minor male attendant of one of the lords. Immediately, she'd stopped rigidly, ignoring my own whisper to ignore it. In the next instant, she'd swept over to the hapless man, and in a display of strength I'd never expected from her, had smashed him against the wall. Holding him there with both hands, she'd shouted, "Never speak to her that way again! Never!" Cowering, the thoroughly overwhelmed man had replied that he would not.

"Tell her you're sorry for it!" Mrs. Goldwell had then demanded, still pressing him to the wall.

"I'm sorry," he'd managed to say, his terrified face looking around her shoulder at me.

I'd went and touched Mrs. Goldwell's arm in a calming way, requesting that she release him. She'd then complied, but only by shoving him sideways, throwing him to the floor. "Dog!" she'd then called him with disgust.

The door he'd been standing beside had then opened, and a surprised gentleman had looked out and seen the man, on the verge of tears, sprawled on the floor. He'd stared at us in confusion and asked what was happening.

"Nothing at all," Mrs. Goldwell had answered, before smoothly taking my arm and leading me away.

When my astonishment had receded a little, I'd said, "I didn't know you're so strong!"

"I am." She'd then told me that she'd been the one who had lifted my mother back and forth from her bed during her final illness. "The duchess was good to me, and I'll never forget it. You've been kind, too. I'm here whenever you have need of me."

I'd appreciated her loyalty, but the display had been a little intimidating for me. Fortunately, no one else had been near enough to see it, and it had been so embarrassing for the man that he'd not spoken of it afterward. It had been the type of thing that drew attention in a way I always avoided, and I hadn't wanted to experience again. Although I hadn't avoided Mrs. Goldwell afterwards, neither had I sought her out for anything. When we encountered each other, I would always stop and exchange a few pleasant words, but nothing more.

The afternoon she saw the ring, we'd just done so, right before one of the kitchen stewards approached me to ask what foods the queen wanted sent to her rooms that night. When the steward heard prunes and dried apricots were included, he gave a little smirk and said, "I suppose Her Majesty gets the same problems as the rest of us, sometimes."

Suddenly the kitchen behind him, with its ovens, fireplaces, and cooks rushing about seemed a chaotically dangerous place. I barely ever commented on the queen to anyone, especially not servants, for things were easily misinterpreted. But I was concerned I might not be understanding something about the order, and asked the steward what he meant.

Before he could answer, Mrs. Goldwell said, "The fruits are used for constipation. He's saying that he thinks that's what the queen wants them for. Because she's constipated."

The steward laughed outright, and replied breezily, "You said it, not me!"

At once, Mrs. Goldwell started to say in a bristling way, "Don't you dare —"

"No, it's fine — everything's fine!" I said quickly. "They're included only because the queen wanted something sweet that wasn't pastry. It's so difficult to have anything fresh in winter." I waved my hand dismissively; too late, I saw the ring in the kitchen light.

Abruptly, Mrs. Goldwell became silent, losing interest in and dropping her confrontation with the steward. As I turned to leave, I heard her hurriedly discuss her own errand with him, and then I was aware she was following me. In the passage right outside the kitchen, she grabbed my hand with the ring and held it close to her face as she studied it. Her eyes then rose to meet my own. "You've never had this before. I know you've no jewellery other than what your mother left you, and I saw what that was. This wasn't part of it."

I could have just walked away, for I had no obligation to her. But I felt I shouldn't. "It's new."

We waited while two women, laughing and chatting, indifferently passed us and went into the kitchen. "It looks very expensive," she continued. "You couldn't have afforded it."

"A friend gave it to me," I answered evasively. "I do have some friends here."

"It's an engagement ring." Although her eyes were still questioning, she said it with certainty.

But I wasn't ready to tell anyone of my marriage plans, even someone so loyal to me. I withdrew my hand from her grasp and hurried away — a curt response, but that would convey the message that I didn't want to talk about it. In future, I'd be careful not to wear the ring until I was closer to Thomas's apartment.

Somehow, I wasn't surprised that night when I returned from visiting Thomas, and, despite the lateness of the hour, found Mrs. Goldwell waiting in my rooms. My hopes that she'd soon forget the incident had been in vain. I should have known that her genuine concern for me — so much greater than mere curiosity — would only increase as she thought about it. As soon as I laid eyes upon her sitting in my outer room, she returned my look of exasperation with one of frank tenacity, and I was certain that this time she wouldn't be put off.

She and my servants knew each other, all having been part of my mother's household, although with different statuses. At Whitehall Palace, because of the multitude of staff, those defined positions and their interactions were more relaxed and varied than in a smaller establishment, and the three of them had been convivially playing at dice while waiting for me. But as soon as I entered, the roles shifted again, my servants retreating into the background while Mrs. Goldwell advanced to a position closer to being my friend.

"I'd like to talk with you," she said.

Wordlessly, I motioned for her to follow me into the other room. Before I left, I told the servants to open the window behind them for air, as the weather was mild. I wasn't one who believed there was harm in the night air, and my request wasn't unusual. But tonight, my reason was that with it open, there was less chance of them being able to hear what we were saying on the other side of the door, which I now closed behind me. Although I knew they weren't inclined to listen, I wouldn't take the chance of them overhearing anything.

I led Mrs. Goldwell to the far side of the bedroom to diminish the possibility even further. "It's about the ring, isn't it?" I asked in a low voice.

"Yes," she answered, equally quietly.

I pointed to the door, indicating the servants beyond it. "You didn't mention it to them, did you?"

"No. I didn't say why I wanted to see you. I didn't ask them anything, either, but they told me where you were. They said you've been teaching Spanish to the sergeant porter. That you've been going there for about an hour almost every night, after the queen has retired and you've completed your duties."

She knew she could only press me so far with questions, although she clearly had more. When she stopped speaking, her face continued to ask them.

Her sincerity deserved an answer. "I'm not teaching him Spanish. He's been showing me how to play cards instead."

Mrs. Goldwell gave a small sound of acknowledgment, as though recognising a believable reason. "He's a widower, isn't he?"

"Yes."

"And he's the one who gave you that ring?"

I withdrew it from my pocket. "Yes."

She stood silently as I held it out for her to see again, then went and opened the cabinet, unlocked the box and placed it inside.

"Is it an engagement ring?"

"Yes. Thomas — Mr. Keyes — and I intend to marry in a month or so. But you mustn't speak a word of it to anyone; it can't be known for some time yet. Preferably not until I'm with child. I'm thought capable of having one. I've consulted a doctor and he's confident it's possible."

A long moment passed before she said, "Your mother would approve. Yes, she would. But why Keyes? He's a good enough man, but for you, shouldn't it be a nobleman?"

"That would threaten the queen. She'd find some way to do to me what she did to Catherine. She's not going to like it, no matter who it is. But there's more chance that she'll accept someone not involved in politics."

"Are you in love with him?" She asked it as though it would be a detriment if I said I was. I could tell she was thinking that I might have been dazzled by some fantasy. If she thought Thomas was taking advantage of me, I had little doubt that she was capable of going to his apartment in a rage and throwing him to the floor, despite his size.

But the question was easily answered. "No. And he's not in love with me, either. We like and respect each other, but this marriage is for ambition. We want to have a child who could follow the queen on the throne. I was told by the doctor to choose a husband who stood straight and tall to reduce the chances of my condition being passed to a child. I've been fortunate indeed to find someone available of such excellent moods also."

She stood utterly still, like a tall, thin tree usually invisible in the surrounding forest, but with deep roots that kept it from being affected by any winds. Then, she repeated, "Your mother would approve."

"I'm a Tudor as much as the queen is. I've an obligation to make the most of it."

"And you're not a ninny like Catherine, who wasted it. Your mother would be proud of you."

"We must be who we are," I said with sudden, passionate certainty. "All of us."

"Keep your voice down," Mrs. Goldwell quickly reminded me. She then moved a little closer to the door and laughed loudly enough to be overheard if the servants were listening, to reset the tone if they'd heard my strong remark. It was then that I knew the extent to which she could be depended upon. Her name, I thought fleetingly, should have been Goldmine instead of Goldwell, for she would be of as much value to me.

She came nearer to me. "I'll help you in whatever way I can."

I knew I had to be honest about the dangers involved. "There could be trouble for you already, in even knowing of this. There's much at stake, for many, many people, most of whom wouldn't want us to succeed."

With contempt, she said, "You mean like the Countess of Lennox, with those stupid sons she's so proud of? Or that selfish woman who's queen in Scotland and wants to take Elizabeth's throne here? She lost her position as the Queen of France, and it's said that was through her own doing. Wait and see — she'll lose the Scottish throne as well, sooner or later. They forget who they are, people like Mary Stuart. She thinks she's cleverer than everyone else, and that God allows her to do whatever she wishes. And it won't be long before things shift for Lord Darnley. We all know what he's like. She'll get rid of him once she sees it herself. And if they're already married, there won't be any way for him to even try to get away, especially if they have a child with a claim to Elizabeth's throne. His fate would be sealed for him. I almost pity him, even though I don't like him."

I'd had no idea that she held such a poor view of people with claims to the throne. If she felt that way, there had to be many others who did as well, those who, like her, worked every day so that the country would exist — farmers, tradesmen, servants, bankers and merchants. They were those who cared little about whether someone was Catholic or Reformed.

"You don't see me as the same as them," I said, "even though they're my relatives."

"You're different. So is the sergeant porter. Any child of yours would make a fine king — one that all the people, the commoners, would want to succeed the queen."

"Any child of mine wouldn't be like Mary Stuart or Lord Darnley."

"I'll continue to assist you. In time, others should also."

I saw that she would. "But remember, there are many who won't want me to succeed in this. I repeat, you must say absolutely nothing of it to anyone." I remembered Thomas had asked me to find a female companion to bring to the ceremony with me. "Can I ask that you attend the wedding with me? We can't repeat the mistake Catherine made in not having enough people present. And if asked about it afterward — which without a doubt you would be — can you say that you saw it? Like I said, it might make trouble for you."

"I don't care," she replied resolutely. "Of course I'll attend."

I knew she would keep her word. She might not have been able to understand or explain it, but I sensed that she considered it an opportunity to do something meaningful, by participating in events that might bring forth the next king or queen.

When we opened the door again for her to leave, the dice game had been resumed by the servants. Without hesitation, Mrs. Goldwell went to the table, took up the dice and shook them and tossed them down. But I returned to my bedroom before seeing how they fell.

In the morning, my serving woman, untypically, asked me a question beyond everyday matters. "What happened to the puppy Lord Darnley gave you?"

I told her that he'd found a good home with the sergeant porter's family in Lewisham.

"It would have been too much for us to have kept him," she replied, a little wistfully. "But it would have been nice to."

I wanted to tell her that if things went as I hoped, we'd all eventually find ourselves living with that puppy in Lewisham. But I knew I couldn't — not yet.

8

I was waiting in Thomas's apartment, the table in the front room ready for a small midday dinner, when he brought his brother and four children up from the Water Gate, where he'd met them upon their arrival. His sister had remained in Lewisham, as the Thames wherries only accommodated five passengers. Exceptions sometimes were made for children, but the youngest son and daughter, between five and ten, were large for their ages. The two older ones, both adolescents, were already nearly as tall as Thomas. His brother also stood head-to-head with him, and I little doubted the sister who'd remained home did also. That this familial height could be repeated in my own child seemed even more likely when I learned, after subtly asking during our first moments of conversation, that their mother had been smaller than average.

Thomas introduced me simply as Lady Mary, without my last name, which his brother and older children might have recognised. I was, he said, a friend who'd graciously arranged the dinner for them. There was no mention of my being the queen's cousin or one of her attendants. I could see they'd been told of my condition before arriving, for only the younger children showed any signs of being in the presence of the unusual, though their interest was barely noticeable — a response that spoke of kindness and good manners. They were also distracted by the novelty of a rare visit to the palace. Spring had come early, and their nearly hour-long trip up the Thames from Deptford on that mid-April morning would have been between newly green riverbanks with the accompanying scent carried on the river breezes. Thomas had promised to show them the palace, especially the presence room where the queen had her main throne, the large central garden, and the great hall where the entire court gathered to dine every day.

"Can we see where the tournament was?" the younger son asked before their cloaks had been removed.

"A little later," Thomas answered. "When I participated, Lady Mary saw the entire spectacle from the stands." In response, all of them, including the children's uncle, requested a full description, which I promised to give at dinner. Meanwhile, Thomas said they could content themselves with seeing his apartment, which the younger children barely remembered. "But don't bother the porters," he warned as they rushed in.

For the occasion, I'd used the parlour as a pantry, from which the specially arranged dishes from the palace kitchen would be served, by porters temporarily employed as waiters. The elder son hurried after his siblings, while his uncle told Thomas, unapologetically, "They're thrilled to be here."

"I've missed them," he said. "Always, I miss them. But I have my position here, for their benefit." Fleetingly, his remark reminded me of his concern that his wife might have thought him lacking in ambition for them. Most likely what she'd said had been misinterpreted by him, for he'd achieved a notable place in life, but such notions weren't always easily discarded.

I turned to the elder daughter, who'd stayed with us. "Everyone is so nicely dressed," I said. All of their clothing was of good quality, well-tailored, and neatly worn. "Your influence, perhaps?"

In addition to being tall, the young woman, about fifteen, had a good appearance, as did all of the children, with the same colouring as their father. "My aunt's," she replied. "We wanted her to come today, but she said no, so as not to require a second wherry. But it was only an excuse, I'm sure. She's ageing and tires easily. She'll enjoy a day of peace and quiet in the house all alone."

I smiled as though I understood. "I'd have liked to meet her. Another time, then." It was a good sign of the woman being unlikely to resent the addition of her brother's second wife to the household.

The other children returned, asking if they might go up to the roof deck. Feeling I should display initiative to show Thomas I'd be capable of it in their home, I suggested they all go while I attended to the first courses of the dinner, which we'd have shortly. When the oldest daughter offered to stay and help, I said the view from the deck was a splendid one, especially on so fine a day, and shouldn't be missed, so she followed the others to the stairs. But it was only half my reason for shooing her away; the other was not wanting her to see my inexperience in managing the dinner. I'd never arranged a meal for so large a group, only one or two occasional guests in my own rooms, which my servants had attended to.

I'd had Mrs. Goldwell advise me not only on the choice of dishes but how to time the serving of them. The kitchen staff were agreeable to preparing special meals for courtiers if the food was paid for and, more importantly, if they were tipped sufficiently, which I'd done. Being seen as regularly in the kitchen as I was also helped, and the dishes had been expertly prepared and ready a few minutes before Thomas's family had arrived. Following Mrs. Goldwell's advice, I'd placed the covered metal trays near the parlour stove until they were about to be served. The first course was salmon and white herring, the second was several sweet dishes, including gingerbread and custards, and the last, roasted hens and blackbird pies.

A quick review showed me everything was ready to be served. There was more than enough of everything, the trays filled to overflowing, which had been noticed by the porters with satisfaction, for they'd already been told the leftovers would be theirs. As I once more repeated instructions for them, I was startled by the unfamiliar sound of running about and playing on the deck overhead. But the porters barely seemed to notice it, as though it were a usual part of life. My anxiety, temporarily abated by seeing the foods were in order, returned at the thought of my having responded with concern to something they saw as commonplace enough to ignore. For the first time, my everyday life felt not only different, but deficient. Getting through the meal ahead began to seem impossible. I should have readied myself for it by rehearsing possible things to talk about. Palace matters, politics, and religion were easy for me, but today such things were irrelevant.

I returned to the front room just in time to hear the roof door flung open, and an avalanche of footsteps echo down the stairs, accompanied by laughter and talking. In that moment I remembered that I'd already successfully spoken with them all when they'd arrived. I grasped that thread of confidence as I showed them all to their places at the table, and called for the porters to serve the first course.

When they were seated, I took my place at the far end of the table, hoping to fade into the background. But at once, Thomas complimented my forethought on seeing that cutlery had been provided. Having thought that a family with so many children might not bring their own, as was common, I'd arranged for loans of sufficient spoons and knives from a palace steward.

They were of fine silver, and the older daughter commented that they looked as though they were used by the queen herself. "We have silver at home, but we seldom use it," she said to me. "You must think us very important, to deserve it." I answered that I did, causing her to smile shyly as she thanked me and said that pewter would have been fine. But when I tried to think of some way to continue the brief exchange, I couldn't. I suddenly felt as though I knew nothing of even the most ordinary aspects of life.

They chatted among themselves about the view from the deck while the fish and side dishes were served, which were met with everyone's approval. Although I barely spoke, I began to relax, my fears of having possibly chosen the wrong foods receding. I still felt separate, not fitting in, but it was a role I was used to, and things were not as difficult as I'd expected in my awkward moments before the meal. In time, things would have to change as I became part of the family, but today I was content to stay as I was.

As the porters cleared away the first course and we waited for the second, the youngest son turned to me and asked, "Can you tell us about the tournament now?"

Nearly in unison, everyone else requested the same as they all looked at me. It felt strange for neither my condition nor my being the queen's cousin to be the cause of my receiving attention. I was being seen as no different from anyone else.

"There were three challengers and more than twenty knights," I began, pushing aside my hesitancy, "all in wonderful costumes, and riding what must have been some of the best horses in the country."

Slowly, I described the event, everyone's rapt attention increasing my self-assurance with each new detail I provided. The porters were taking a bit longer than I'd expected to bring in the sweet courses, but with my attention diverted the delay didn't concern me. Somehow, they arrived just when I felt I had nothing further to say. "And you'll all be proud to hear that your father did very well indeed in it," I finished.

"Although I didn't win," Thomas added, making a silly face of disappointment.

"Sometimes," his brother said, "it's not the winning, but being a part of it that matters."

But as the porters began to serve the sweet dishes, and Thomas reminded the children not to overindulge as the final, most substantial course would follow, I felt satisfied that I had won some small tournament of my own right here at the table. With newfound ease, I told the porters to leave the dishes, and that I would attend to any further serving required.

After the meal was over, I finished with the porters while Thomas showed the children the palace. They were then all tucked into a wherry for their trip home, and I returned to my rooms. Even with my servants there, they seemed empty in a way they never had before. But the stillness and quiet in no way altered my satisfaction with how the day had gone. When the family had departed, they'd pleaded with me to accompany their father home for Easter the following week, which I'd have liked to agree to, but I knew it wasn't wise for us to be seen so much together. The time would come for me to visit the house in Lewisham, but not yet. Until then, the day's visit would suffice as a glimpse of what my future there could be.

As I went into my bedroom, I thought with amusement of some of the children's antics after dinner when they'd been eager to see the palace. A moment later, the serving woman stood in the open doorway, looking in. "Is everything all right, my lady?"

"Yes. Why?"

"You seemed to call or cry out."

It must have been that I'd laughed aloud over what I'd just been thinking of. "It's nothing. Thank you." She closed the door as she left, leaving me with the uncomfortable knowledge that laughter from me was unrecognisable for her. It was something that might change in the future, if things continued on the same path.

It was then that I remembered her talking about the puppy recently, and I realised I'd completely forgotten to ask Thomas's children how he was. I'd be sure to the next time I saw them, which I hoped wouldn't be too far away. I'd thoroughly enjoyed the day with them, being Lady Mary, instead of Lady Mary Grey. But it was important for me not to forget that it was only because I was Lady Mary Grey that I'd met them at all. The date for Thomas and I to marry would have to be set as soon as Easter was over.

The next day another of my cousins, Henry Hastings, Earl of Huntington, came to court to see the queen. He was not a Tudor but descended from the brother of the last of the earlier Yorkist kings, whose daughter had been my great-grandmother. However, his claim to the throne was still important. When my sister Jane had been married to the son of the scheming Duke of Northumberland, Lord Henry had at the same time been married to that duke's daughter. Since she was sister to Robert Dudley, who had such influence over the queen, his status had improved greatly in the first years of Elizabeth's reign. But when three years ago the queen's death had been thought imminent, a faction had favoured his claim instead of my sister Catherine's. If the queen had not recovered, he might very well have become king.

The queen, upon learning of it, had been outraged at such presumption, despite her attachment to Lord Robert, and had shown her disappointment that the young earl had allowed his royal descent to be used in such a way. Although not fully exiled from court, he'd been relegated to the ranks of those not considered for official positions that would increase their power and wealth. Since then, he had rarely appeared at court at all, and when his wife had, the queen had been ungracious to her. Today's visit, during Easter week when the queen was thought to be in a generous mood, was undoubtedly an attempt to improve their standing.

He arrived in black clothes of the severe style worn by those of more extreme Reformed beliefs, which he'd aligned with as soon as the queen had succeeded her Catholic sister. Although it was said that his faith was sincere and not the opportunism it was for so many, it made him an attractive candidate for the succession for many with political motives. His choice of clothes for the visit, despite being a statement of religion, could be interpreted as political as well — and a mistake, if he was attempting to win back the queen's favour. They also made him look older than his thirty or so years, his fair face and hair in startling contrast to the blackness of his coat and plain hat as he walked purposefully across the outer room towards the queen's inner apartments, where the doors opened and closed behind him.

Everyone at court knew that the longer an audience with the queen took, the better the outcome for those meeting with her. It was immediately clear that the earl hadn't been well received when after a surprisingly short time the doors opened again and he reemerged, his face bearing exactly the same look it had when he'd gone in. Ignoring the stares of the courtiers, he moved towards the outer corridor door, which right then opened to admit the Countess of Lennox, on her way to the queen.

Both stopped, as though confronting each other, two of the most prominent Reformed and Catholic sympathisers in the country. Their unspoken dislike of each other was obvious behind the thin veil of courtesy and court protocol. For an instant they remained so, unyielding, each blocking the other's path. Throughout the room, silence prevailed, the sight of my two cousins a stark reminder of all of the religious troubles that still existed in the country. I knew then that the earl's choice of clothing had been deliberate, a demonstration of the future he could bring, as much as the countess's recent appearance with her second son had been. In every audience the queen granted, there was calculation and subtle intent. The complexity and importance of the issues she contended with required unwavering alertness, and she needed to be acutely aware of the reverberations of any decision she made. It was no wonder she responded with such anger when taken by surprise, for underneath were great responsibilities most people knew nothing of.

The earl bowed, and the countess curtsied. "Countess," he said formally.

"My lord," she replied in the same tone. He stepped to the left and she to the right, and each swept past the other, one towards the queen and the other away, both vanishing through the opposing doors.

Mrs. Parry had been inside during the earl's audience. A little later, when she came out, I asked what had happened.

"The queen refused his request for rooms at court again, for himself and his wife. Had she said yes, he might have had other things to ask for as well. But she was distant from the start, barely offering him a welcome. He saw it was useless to continue and made a quick exit." She said it as though it was something that he should have expected. "This queen's not one to easily forgive," she continued. "Your sister's learning that the unfortunate way."

"Do you think the queen would have given her permission to marry if she'd asked?" I asked slowly.

"Difficult to say. Maybe, maybe not. It didn't help that Catherine chose a man with such political importance."

As Mrs. Parry smiled mildly and walked away, I reminded myself that Thomas had no political significance whatsoever. For the first time, I considered what had until now seemed the impossible option of asking the queen if I could marry him. Not doing so was backing her into a corner where she'd have no choice but to be angry and try to refuse to accept it, as she'd done to Catherine. Until now my plan had assumed this outcome, to be countered by careful planning that provided no possibility of having the marriage overturned. But today's spectacle of the continuing lack of favour of the Earl of Huntington over something which couldn't have even been discussed beforehand, was making me reconsider. Possibly, just possibly, it might be best to ask the queen first.

Most days after midday dinner, she returned to her apartments with many of her gentlewomen for an hour or so of quiet informality. At times she was approached then by those seeking her help or approval for marriages or other family matters, often successfully, for it was one of the few occasions when she showed anything resembling sisterly accord with her attendants, and sympathy for their hopes and ambitions. If a gentlewoman was seen to go and kneel before her, it was understood that such a request was forthcoming, and the others would move away while she spoke. If I did the same, it would afford her the opportunity of hearing me alone, without the pressure of counsellors or anyone with motivations of their own. The setting would also present the marriage as a domestic matter rather than a political one. She would, of course, understand that it was, but perhaps not that my motive was to have a child who could be heir to her throne. She might believe only that I wanted to marry Thomas, and have a life with him.

All through dinner I continued to think of it, ignoring the idle talk around me at my table, and barely remembering to acknowledge Thomas at his. When I did, I was reassured by his presence, even at a distance. Surely the queen would find him acceptable in ways that Catherine's husband, an earl, hadn't been. At worst, if asked she could only say no, and as I looked at her seated on the dais even further away from me than Thomas, I thought that if so, it would leave us in much the same position as if I hadn't asked at all.

Still undecided, I followed the other gentlewomen back to the queen's inner apartments, and went into a sitting room with them. I seldom did so, usually attending to matters of my own at that time, and my presence was noticed by some of them, including Mrs. Parry, who offered me a smile of welcome. More importantly, I saw the queen look at me, before quickly turning away. Anxiety jabbed at me; she knew it was uncommon for me to be there. It was entirely possible that she already expected I was there for a reason. I went to the far side of the room and stood against the wall, where I could see her from one side, but she wouldn't see me unless she turned.

She was sitting in the very middle of the room with all the women surrounding her, mostly standing and at varying distances. They were in groups of two or more as they chatted among themselves in low voices, still very much aware of the queen's central presence. Two of the youngest hovered on either side of her, holding her attention with whatever they were describing in a very lively manner. The queen responded, saying something inaudible to me, but making one woman beckon to another further off, who joined them and said something else to the queen, causing her to laugh in a carefree way that made everyone in the room look at her. If her mood was as easy as it seemed, it boded well for a positive response to my request. But I remained where I stood. No matter how friendly her manner was with the other gentlewomen, for me it wouldn't be the same.

The queen laughed again, and I took a deep breath and walked to another part of the room, behind her, where she couldn't see me at all. From there, she somehow looked more formidable, as though her ease with the gentlewomen was merely a mask of conviviality. I moved again, to a place opposite where I'd stood at first, and viewed the queen from another angle. The two women who'd been with her earlier, and the third who'd joined them, were gone, replaced by two others, standing and listening to her. I was about to go forward, but the queen suddenly turned sideways and fixed her green eyes on me in a powerful stare.

Perhaps it was only by chance that she did so, or perhaps she somehow sensed that I was there and I wanted something. If she hadn't turned, I almost certainly would have at least attempted to put forward my request. But her stare was overwhelming, far beyond uninviting. What she'd done to Catherine and the Earl of Huntington, she was capable of doing to me, or any of our cousins, be it the Countess of Lennox or Lord Darnley, or even Mary Queen of Scots, if we opposed her. For all that the expression on her face said nothing, the message in her stare was not to be mistaken. She would tolerate us only so long as she could control us. All of us had claims to her throne, but who occupied it after her would be decided by her alone.

I curtsied respectfully, in deferential acknowledgment of her looking at me. I started to lose my balance, as my condition occasionally caused to happen, but was able to steady myself. Then I managed to subtly return her unnerving stare with one pretending casual indifference. She turned away, and I moved back where I'd been behind her, on the far side of the room by the wall, the type of place I was used to.

Later, at his apartment, I told Thomas, "It was fortunate I didn't ask, for I'm sure now she would have said no. It was foolish of me to even consider that she might say yes. We need to stay with what we've planned all along." The deck of cards sat unused on the table between us. "When she finds out, she's not going to like it. I need to know you're absolutely aware of that. If you want to change your mind, and don't want to go any further, I'll understand. It's much for me to ask of you."

He reached across the table and touched the engagement ring on my finger. "When I gave you this, I knew what was ahead. I knew my commitment would have to equal your determination, which leaves me in awe sometimes. How strong you were, to have even considered trying to ask her like that! It's not an easy thing to do. I've seen powerful men arriving at the palace for an audience with her, who looked like they'd have preferred to run away instead. Of course I haven't changed my mind."

"You may even be removed from your position here. But once it's known the marriage is valid, it should make a difference — especially if I'm with child by then."

"Pray God for it," he said smoothly, in a way that sounded like he was sure it was a prayer that would be answered.

"We might both be sent from court for a time. You'd likely go to Lewisham, and me to some distant relative of mine. But it wouldn't look good for the queen, either to her subjects or foreigners, to have two of her cousins in the same circumstances for too long. It would suggest that she can't control her own family, let alone the country. Eventually, we'd be restored. And then, great benefits could follow — for a child, of course, but for us as well."

"I'm to go to Lewisham on Sunday for Easter, but I'll return that day. On Monday I'll speak to the minister I've found about when the ceremony can take place. We should be married the following week, or the one after."

Since last January when I'd set my plan in motion, all the required pieces had appeared and smoothly gone into place as though mysteriously guided to it. It was a sign that good fortune was with us and that any future obstacles would be overcome. Surely success would follow, and within a year I might be holding the child who could one day become king or queen. But as I left Thomas's apartment, what I kept thinking of was how the queen had stared at me earlier that day.

In Scotland, it seemed that Mary Stuart and Lord Darnley had been waiting for Easter to pass for the same reason that Thomas and I had been. On Good Friday, there began to be whispers at court that the queen was angry over news she'd received. "It's about Mary Stuart and Lord Darnley," Mrs. Parry told me quietly when I was able to speak to her alone in the queen's outer room. "They intend to go ahead with their marriage without the queen's permission. It's a major offence, since Darnley's an English subject. The queen has ordered him to stop immediately and return here. But it's said their betrothal has already been announced." She nodded towards the Countess of Lennox across the room, for once not in the inner apartment, and seated alone as though the courtiers were already avoiding her. "Wait and see — it won't be long before she's in trouble too over this. No one's going to believe she didn't have something to do with it, especially not the queen. Even though it's likely that it's what the queen has wanted all along, she'll now make a show of taking it out on the countess, the only one of them within her reach here. My bet would be that she ends up in the Tower before this is over. Or it could even be something —" she hesitated — "beyond that. Unlikely, but it could be. You never know what the queen's going to do about anything. It's one of the ways she's able to keep things the way she wants them."

After she left me, I took a seat where I could see the countess. The mention of her possibly being sent to the Tower had affected me with a vague dread in a way I wouldn't have expected. I'd never been there, the queen not having gone to the royal apartments there during the time I'd been in attendance on her. It was a place I'd have preferred to never set foot in. My executed father's and sister Jane's remains were buried there. Catherine had escaped execution but been held there for years as well. Such could be the results for anyone who opposed those who sat on the throne.

Across the room, the countess sat reading a book, almost certainly one of prayers. Despite her Catholic sympathies, I was sure it was a Reformed text of the moderate type most closely coinciding with religion as followed by the queen, chosen in case any courtiers passed close enough to see it. There was a quiet, steady look about her as she held it, almost as though she was oblivious to her deteriorating political position and the empty seats near her. Even the previous day they would have been filled with those seeking to benefit by association with one so often the queen's companion. And yet she seemed resigned to her isolation, in a way that left me wondering if it was her ambition that supported her, and if so, to what extent she could rely on it. Without question, her son being married to the Queen of Scotland would be a crowning achievement for her, along with the possibility of their children succeeding to the English throne. I wondered if she would feel it was worth it if it resulted in her being sent from court to endure years of solitude at some remote country estate, never seeing family or friends. It would not be possible to contest the marriage in Scotland, like Catherine's had been. For the first time, it occurred to me that the only reason Catherine and her husband hadn't been executed had been because the queen had found a way for their marriage to be overturned. But if Thomas and I proceeded as planned, she'd have no way of doing the same to ours.

The difference was that Catherine and her husband, and the countess and her family, were established political figures, while Thomas and I weren't. For a moment, I sat very still, looking at the countess and her prayer book, as though they held some message for me. There was no reason yet to assume that things would turn out badly for her. Her skill at whatever game she played was respected by all. It was fully possible that by Sunday she wouldn't be in the Tower but instead seated by the queen's side at the Easter celebrations.

On Easter Sunday morning, when I arrived to take my place with the gentlewomen assembling for the first prayer service, the countess wasn't present. There was also a noticeable air of tension as the gentlewomen whispered to each other in little groups. It wasn't long before I overheard the reason: the countess had been ordered to remain in her rooms for having received letters from Mary Stuart and opening and reading them without giving them first to the queen, which as a subject she was required to do with any message from a foreign ruler. That those letters had specifically been about plans for her son's wedding had angered the queen and caused her to take immediate steps. The only reason the countess hadn't yet been sent to the Tower for treason was because the queen's advisors felt they should wait to see if the action taken would be a sufficient deterrent to delay the wedding while further diplomacy to stop it took place.

Immediately the dread I'd felt previously became more pronounced. Mrs. Parry wasn't wrong about a stay in the Tower being possible for the countess, and maybe even worse, if Lord Darnley's marriage wasn't stopped. The queen had already amply demonstrated that family connections were never sufficient to prevent her protecting herself from anyone she saw as reaching for her throne, either at present or in the future.

At Westminster Abbey, I was barely able to listen to the sermon. Only a few days earlier, the queen had piously washed the feet of several poor women there, as was customary before Easter. But she'd done so wearing a splendid black gown and headdress and jewellery, in striking contrast to the rags worn by the poor women, which for me had rendered the ritual ridiculous and meaningless. It was entirely possible that for her any real Christian values — Reformed or Catholic — had been subordinated by her concerns for her own security. She could never be expected to sympathise with anyone who displeased her because she saw herself mirrored in no one. She simply didn't care what happened to Catherine, the Earl of Huntington, the Countess of Lennox, or me.

The breakfast that followed at Whitehall was the first after Lent, and delicious foods not usually served had been prepared. Easter was when the best clothing was worn, and the Great Hall was full of courtiers elegantly dressed in new garments. After breakfast when the queen went into the large central garden, they followed, their colourful attire flowing like a wave of late April flowers around her on the paths. As I walked behind, I saw the beauty of the garden with its statues, fountains and spring foliage in ways I never had before. Whitehall and the other palaces were magnificent buildings, the centres of anything of importance in the country. Residing in them as a member of the queen's household, my life was a comfortable one and could continue to be so. But the marriage I was set upon would undoubtedly change that in ways that might be permanent, whether I had a child or not. All reports indicated that Catherine found the separation from court nearly as difficult as being parted from her husband. No two sisters could be more different than we were, but our fates could be similar. Although at court I was in the background, I'd been there for several years and had become used to it. To throw it all away for a dream might be a very foolish thing to do.

"We should delay for a while," I told Thomas that night. "Until today, I'd thought the possibility of a marriage between my cousins in Scotland would serve as a distraction from ours here, and that when ours became known it would be viewed leniently by comparison because of the lack of politics involved. But now, I think it might be the opposite, and a strident response from the queen is more likely. She's angry at the countess. What I heard is that the countess tried to bring the letters to the queen right after she read them, but she wouldn't even see her. It's best that we wait to see if that marriage is stopped, and if not, what the mood is here afterward."

"I'm disappointed," he said, the expression on his face saying the same. "All day today in Lewisham I thought of how it's going to be to have you in my house. It's the right place for you, seeing to a large household."

"I couldn't have come immediately," I reminded him. "After our marriage, we have to go on as we are for a time. Eventually I'll be there; I anticipate it as eagerly as you. But for now, we should wait."

"You know better about all of this than I do. If you think it, you're right. But you agree that our engagement continues, don't you? With that, I can wait."

"Yes, we can go on as we have been. It's only a matter of choosing the right moment."

It was reassuring that he wasn't taking the opportunity to withdraw from the commitment. He was a fine person, exactly the type of husband I'd hoped to find. But later that night, as I sat alone in my own room, I wondered how he'd respond if I had to tell him our plans would come to nothing.

9

For a month, there was a stalemate over Lord Darnley's wedding, with the countess remaining in her rooms while the border was closely watched for any attempted exchange of correspondence. Meanwhile, other news from Scotland told of opposition to the marriage by many lords for being too favourable to the Catholic party, and because of the pride and arrogance of Lord Darnley. In England, the queen's advisors discussed the possible effects of the marriage on English politics and concluded it shouldn't take place. Formal letters were sent through ambassadors stating so, and asking Mary to choose a husband from any other English nobleman or foreign prince. Instead, she created Lord Darnley the Earl of Ross, a clear indication their marriage would go ahead.

"He shouldn't have accepted the title without asking the queen here first," I told Thomas as we sat playing cards in our usual places at the table. We'd resumed the games which had before Easter gradually stopped and been replaced by conversation. Starting again felt like a deliberate way of avoiding speculating about how things would go for us in the future, which was mostly what we'd talked about before. Since there was now a chance it would all have been for nothing, it would be cruel and unfair to him for me to continue as though nothing had changed. Although the plan still hadn't been entirely discarded, with every passing day it receded further. What was happening to the countess was impossible to ignore. The deterioration of the situation in Scotland promised no good outcome for her, with a stay in the Tower seeming more and more likely unless she found some way of appeasing the queen. But the actions of her son and future daughter-in-law were making that impossible.

"Darnley's an English subject and his allegiance is first to Elizabeth," Thomas answered. "An earldom in Scotland divides it. Now the queen here and her advisors have even more reason for taking their position. Mary and Darnley were foolish to do it."

"They wouldn't have, if the countess had been able to advise them. The queen knew she had to prevent it. There may be a strategy behind what she's been doing. If she can claim that she was displeased with the marriage because of politics, she has a reason to refuse both of them as possible successors."

"Our marriage isn't political at all," said Thomas, smiling in a satisfied way. "That argument can't be used against us by anyone."

"The queen is skilled at getting what she wants," I said evasively. "We shouldn't forget it." To change the subject, I asked him who'd arrived at the Water Gate that day, and we continued our card game as he told me of all the palace's comings and goings.

At the beginning of June, one of the English ambassadors returned from Scotland with the news that although the marriage there was being announced, it would be delayed in the hopes that further diplomacy would make it acceptable to Queen Elizabeth. For that purpose, a Scottish ambassador specifically chosen by Mary Stuart would arrive by the middle of the month.

Although the returned English ambassador had failed in his mission, he was immediately popular among the courtiers wanting to know more about rumours that Mary was behaving as though deeply in love with Lord Darnley. The younger gentlewomen were especially eager — once they saw that the queen wasn't holding him responsible for the failure of his mission, and that she wouldn't dislike their display of interest in her Scottish counterpart, they swarmed around him. The ambassador held their attention with detailed descriptions of Mary's apparent infatuation with Lord Darnley, who, despite his attractive appearance and manner, was disliked by everyone else. "She seems to see in him what others don't," he told a group while I was close by, "and refuses to listen to anyone suggesting otherwise. When, that is, they have an opportunity to express it, which isn't often, since she keeps Darnley so often at her side. With her, he's charming in a way that looks sincere, not at all aloof or disdainful as he was here, and as he is to almost everyone there when not in Queen Mary's presence. There's something mysterious in how she responds to him, almost as though she sees a reflection of her Tudor self. For his part, no one knows how he really feels about her."

I remembered the fear I'd seen in him on the day we'd encountered each other, and how he'd talked of feeling like a sacrificial lamb, since Mary's first husband was said to have been killed by her. He'd also been sure he was being sent to marry her to further Queen Elizabeth's wish to consolidate the Catholic claims to the succession. Now, I could only wonder if he felt differently after his wonderful reception there. If he was only a puppet being manipulated by the ambitions of others, he certainly had found himself on what seemed like a very fortunate stage.

A gentleman courtier then approached the ambassador and asked about Lord Darnley's father, the Earl of Lennox, and whether he'd been successful in bringing the lords of Scotland together in support of the marriage as beneficial to the country, and themselves individually. This aspect of the situation was of little interest to the gentlewomen, most of whom drifted away from the group. But I stayed nearby, knowing that the game of Scottish politics was as difficult as the English one, and the religious divide as present and complicated.

"Has the earl drawn any of the Reformed lords to them?" the gentleman asked. "Here, he and his wife are seen as Catholic supporters, but perhaps less so there? And it's the countess who's usually seen as such, rather than the earl."

But the ambassador's answer was that the earl hadn't done so, or in any way been able to moderate the unpleasant aspects of Lord Darnley's behaviour. Like I'd thought, no matter what religious alliances she'd maintained, the countess would have been far more successful at establishing the Scottish unity that was going to be necessary for the marriage to not only happen but to be maintained politically. In not allowing her to accompany her family, Queen Elizabeth had known exactly what she was doing.

For the next two weeks, the arrival of the Scottish ambassador was eagerly awaited. During that time, it was announced that a week before the end of the month the queen would start her yearly royal progress around the nearby country, first visiting her other residences, starting with Greenwich Palace. It was understood by everyone that the queen would reach some decision about the Countess of Lennox before the court departed. It was obvious that what the expected ambassador had to say would matter, but day after day passed without his arrival, and the departure date for Greenwich drew closer.

The approaching change of residence was welcome to me, since Thomas as sergeant porter always stayed at Whitehall whether the court was there or not, and my being away would give me time to make up my mind about whether to proceed with my plan or discard it for good. We wouldn't be back until September, except for a stay of one or two days in three weeks' time, when the queen would attend a wedding in the city before moving on again.

I felt it was best to speak directly with Thomas about our reconsidering where things stood in September, and I was waiting until we were close to leaving before doing so. But a week before the departure date, I arrived late in the evening at his apartment to find him still wearing his official clothes and hat. "I have to go down to the gate," he told me. "The Countess of Lennox is being sent to the Tower in one of the queen's barges. She's expected at any moment."

Something close to panic seized me. For the next moment, I could only stand there, not sure of what to say or think. But I knew that what was happening had become likelier and likelier with each day that had passed without the ambassador from Scotland arriving, which, for whatever reason, he had not.

There was a call for Thomas from the stairs in the outer room, and he went and spoke to whoever was there. Then he came back and said, "She's almost here. I have to go. Stay, if you like. It shouldn't take long." I stood listening to his hurried footsteps on the stairs as they gradually grew quieter. Then, suddenly, I followed.

The office below opened into the gallery waiting room one had to cross to the Water Gate steps. The connecting door was open, and I arrived just in time to look through and see the guarded countess and two of her women servants pass by, preceded and followed by palace officials. But instead of looking distraught or frightened, there was an expression of serene triumph on the countess's face, and she walked as though being led not to the Tower but instead to a coronation. It was clear she felt she'd won the game she'd been playing with the queen — and she may have. They reached the Water Gate door and went through to where Thomas would be waiting to assist her into the barge. There was no reason for me to stay, so I turned to go.

Back in the apartment, the parlour window was already open, and I went and looked out to where I determined the barge would pass in the distance before rounding the bend in the Thames. The panic I'd felt earlier was gone. I knew now that before long my cousins in Scotland would not only be married but would also soon have a child who could succeed to the English throne. I also knew that I had to continue trying to have one of my own. I was as much a Tudor as the countess was, and as capable of facing the anger of the queen as her. The alternative of living the rest of my life without having tried was unacceptable. It wasn't too late, and the winner in the game could still be me.

I heard Thomas's approaching footsteps in the corridor. It was unfortunate that I'd hesitated to marry him right after Easter, because if I had, I could already be carrying the child that I so wanted. I turned to the door as he entered, the sight of him again causing me to feel only certainty.

He smiled at me and said, "Oh, good, you stayed." He took off his hat and dropped it on the table. "She's a noble one, that countess. Her serving women looked frightened, but not her. It was like she was simply going for a moonlit ride on the Thames."

He came and stood beside me at the window, and we both looked out. Far below on the river, the lanterns of the barely visible barge showed its progress. "Is that them?" he asked.

"I think it is. It only just appeared."

"There were no other boats about when I left the steps. There's never much traffic at this time."

"Did you hear anything else about it from any of the officials?"

"After they left, two who stayed behind were talking. They said the queen's becoming afraid that after the marriage of Darnley and Mary, the English Catholics are going to try and make them king and queen here. The countess has been sent to the Tower so she can't be a figurehead for them to rally around."

Standing next to him, I felt again the difference in our sizes, which I'd ceased being aware of months ago. He was large and strong in ways I wasn't. I stepped back from the window, and as he turned from it, I looked up at his appealing face and sensed again his ever-present calmness and reliability. Such traits in a child who could become king or queen would be welcomed by all.

"Thomas, it was a mistake for us to delay marrying," I said. "My mistake, not yours, for I know you were ready to. And I'm sorry for the disappointment that you must have felt. I can promise you it won't happen again. But now, what can we do? I know there isn't sufficient time before I have to leave for Greenwich, but I don't want to wait until September." I wanted no chance to lose my nerve again before then. "The court returns here briefly in three weeks for the wedding the queen's attending."

"They've been getting ready for it at Durham House," he answered. "There are going to be all types of festivities, I've been hearing. Barges have been stopping there for weeks with decorations and supplies."

"We'll only be at Whitehall for one or two days, but that could be long enough. I wasn't invited, so I'll be here when they all go."

"They should have included you," he said with concern.

"No doubt they felt the presence of Crouchback Mary would diminish the day."

"Mary —" he began kindly.

"It's nothing. I'm used to it. Now, can we arrange our marriage for then?"

His eyes widened with enthusiasm. "Yes, easily! We'll have it that same day. The families of that bride and groom are both favoured by the queen, so she and her retinue should be at the wedding for half the night, if not more. It's the perfect time for ours. We'll have that night together, and maybe even a second one if we're lucky and the queen wants to stay for another day before moving on. We don't have to wait for September!" He hesitated, as though searching for the right words. "I've quite made up my mind that I want this, you see. If anything were to now stop me from marrying you, I'd regret it for the rest of my life. I'd never have thought it possible, but once it was, it became something I'd always remain incomplete without."

I'd already known his commitment ran deep, but not to this extent. "I, too. Although I wasn't sure of it until tonight."

"We'll have the ceremony right here in this parlour. Very quiet, only a few people, but enough so that it can't be questioned afterward. But for all its simplicity, it'll be so much more meaningful than that elaborate one downriver at Durham House."

"Yes," I agreed. "Those types of celebrations don't matter at all. They're insignificant, soon forgotten. I don't care about any of that."

When I left the apartment a little later, it was with the feeling of purpose and clarity with which I'd first entered it months ago, but hadn't felt for many days.

*

The next afternoon the ambassador finally arrived from Scotland. He was received by the queen in front of several councillors and courtiers so that her display of anger towards him — and my cousins — would be seen and reported, and it wasn't long before I knew of it. The queen had made a pretence of having sent the countess to the Tower because of not knowing how close he'd been, but had gone on to say she'd done so because the countess had broken a previous promise never to marry off her sons without her agreement. As to the actions of Mary and Darnley, she was not only deeply offended but had no understanding of why the recommendations of her, their devoted cousin, should be so ignored. If the ambassador's visit, she'd said, was for anything other than to tell her they'd changed their minds, there'd been no reason for him to have made the trip at all. The fact that she'd known the plans wouldn't be altered had been shown by her then leaving the room without letting him speak.

Over the following days, the queen refused to see him again, or to allow him to go to the Tower to give the countess the letters from her husband and son that he'd brought, or to meet with any of her councillors or officials. Very soon, he decided to leave. Meanwhile, most of the court was preparing for the move to Greenwich Palace. Mrs. Goldwell, though, would remain at Whitehall as she usually did. I waited until the day before our departure after Thomas had spoken to the chosen minister and our wedding date had been set before letting her know. Weeks ago, I'd told her we'd decided to delay, to which she'd replied only that she'd be available whenever I needed.

"So, you'll be married that same night as the wedding at Durham House?" she asked.

"Yes. We don't want to wait until I return in September."

She smiled in a way that suggested she appreciated the contrast between the sincerity of our wedding and the emptiness of the other. She then asked if the sergeant porter knew she'd be attending me, and when I told her he did, she said that she'd go to the apartment before I returned and see that the bed was properly made and everything else was in order. "And what of your nightdress? Have you a new one? It should be finely made."

When I replied that I didn't, she said she'd have one ready for me. I started to express my gratitude, but she stopped me. "Your mother isn't here to see to it, or to ask anyone else to. Go to Greenwich and concern yourself with nothing until you return. Send your servant with a message, should you think of anything else I can do."

In the morning, a small fleet of barges was lined up on the river outside the Water Gate, and the departures for Greenwich began right after breakfast. When I arrived with the queen and her other gentlewomen, Thomas, surrounded by porters, was waiting on the steps, and I watched him bow low to the queen before he came forward and assisted her into the royal barge. As he did, a breeze caused the water to ripple and the barge wobbled slightly. The queen, taken by surprise, touched his elbow for support. But she quickly steadied herself and took her seat, and Thomas bowed again and returned to the steps to guide her chosen companions in. The barge then departed, and the next one for the gentlewomen arrived. Thomas stayed in place to assist us, and as he helped me in, we at the same moment looked directly into each other's faces, a perfectly timed silent farewell.

The barge pulled away, following the queen's down the river. It wasn't long before we passed Durham House, with barges of commerce being unloaded. Under other circumstances, it might have been my wedding being prepared in that grand mansion. If my sister Jane was still queen, Durham House, or any of the other Strand mansions fronting on the Thames, could today have been my husband-to-be's family home. But as I watched what looked like great casks of wine being taken inside, I knew it mattered little that at my wedding there would at best be a simple tankard from the Whitehall cellars. Because of what might come of it, my marriage would still be the more important of the two that day.

The day was fine, the breezes only mild, and the line of barges proceeded smoothly with no repetition of the small river turbulence that had caused the queen to seek Thomas's support as she'd boarded. A little further down, the sight of the Tower as we passed it caused me to remember that it contained the remains of my father and sister. But also within its walls was a doubtlessly still unvanquished Countess of Lennox, and I felt no return of hesitation but only a deep and rightful ambition. I would be married in three weeks. With luck, I would have a child who one day might be travelling down the Thames in the prime position of the royal barge instead of being tucked away among the courtiers in the ones following.

Although Greenwich Palace, like Whitehall, was set on the Thames, it felt very different, being outside the city with a park on its side opposite the river. It was built from brick with rooms arranged in more compact and organised ways that were easier to find one's way around than at Whitehall. Everyone seemed to appreciate the change, for not only had the stay at Whitehall been nearly half a year long by the time we'd left, but due to the season it had been spent mostly indoors. At Greenwich there were beautiful flowers and birds in arrays of different colours everywhere, set against a landscape of rich greenery. The weather was good and nearly entire days were spent outdoors, engaged in games or sports or walking in the gardens or park. Almost immediately the mood of the courtiers became easier and more relaxed, and even the queen appeared to be in good spirits. She smiled more and talked frequently with her attendants and visitors.

My determination to marry Thomas remained unchanged, but as the days passed, I became concerned over something that had previously had no place in my thoughts, which was how he would find me as a wife on our wedding night and thereafter. I already knew what had to happen between a man and a woman for a marriage to be valid, and for any children to be born. I'd overheard conversations between the women courtiers, always with the same descriptions of the main details, so I was sure they were accurate. But what I began to think was that, in that setting, my condition might finally make a difference to Thomas, and become an impediment to our marriage's primary motivation. If so, everything we'd set out to do would have been for nothing.

After several days I decided I was being foolish, for Thomas had been married and would know to expect that my condition wouldn't make me so different from other women. But I found I was still unable to let go of my concerns. I considered seeking an opinion or recommendations in a general way from one of the gentlewomen, but there was no one I'd be comfortable enough with, not even Mrs. Parry. Finally, I remembered Mrs. Goldwell back at Whitehall. There'd be little time for it, but she'd be able to answer my questions and perhaps make suggestions that would restore my confidence.

On the morning we returned to Whitehall, two days before the wedding at Durham House, I sent for her immediately.

"Everything is ready," she told me a little later in my rooms, while my servants were away on errands. I knew this already, for at the Water Gate, I'd lingered behind the other gentlewomen passing through the waiting gallery, and Thomas had been able to quietly tell me that the ceremony would take place at around nine on the set evening after the minister had arrived.

Mrs. Goldwell was holding a cloth bag, from which she now withdrew the nightdress she'd told me she'd have for me. She held it out, and I saw it was of lightweight white linen with delicate lace trim, and widely made so as to allow easy movement within it. Taking it from her, I felt the softness of the fabric and knew it would be comfortable to wear.

"Seeing you again, I'm sure I estimated the size right," she said, taking it back and holding it up against me. "Yes, it should be fine. Try it on tonight and if you want any adjustments, give it to me tomorrow."

There couldn't have been a more appropriate opening for what I wanted to speak to her about. "I have a question," I began hesitantly.

She smiled gently. "I thought you might."

"I know what to expect, from what I've heard in the discussions of women. But I wonder now if my husband is going to find me as attractive as most men find their wives. Attractive enough, I mean. I'm misshapen in ways most women aren't."

"Don't think of it," she said at once. "The sergeant porter must have long ago decided that doesn't matter. Besides, even if he lights a candle, the soft dimness of the room should be a smoothing cover. I assume you can lie on your back with ease?"

"Yes, if I position my pillows so."

"Tell me how, and I'll go in and arrange them for you first on the right side of the bed, so be sure to take it. Undo your hair when you undress, so when you lie down it flows about you on the pillows." She reached over and removed my bonnet. "As I thought, your hair is excellent, wavy and full, and you'll finally have the opportunity to show it. He'll like it, and your wonderful eyes. And you're soft and smooth to the touch, in the way only someone your age can be. Trust me, your husband isn't going to be disappointed by how he finds you. Let him take the lead in this. He's been married, and by all accounts his marriage was a good one. He'll know what to do."

"Thank you. You've been a help to me," I said as my doubts vanished.

"I've placed several fresh linens and another nightdress and robe inside the bedroom cabinet on the middle shelf. There'll be water in the basin, with more in a pitcher. You must already know you'll bleed a little, as you're supposed to, and I think that it's important for other people to see the stained sheet or garment because of who you are. If you like, I can mention to the sergeant porter that the minister and the others should wait to see it afterward in the parlour. It's to make sure the marriage can't be questioned the way your sister's was."

"Yes, please do."

"What do you intend to wear?" she asked as she gave me back my bonnet.

"This." I gestured to my dress, a paler green than the winter livery. "Since we're only here for a few days, my other dresses remain packed and I only have my white livery available. The other gentlewomen going to the Durham House wedding are going to wear it, but since I'm not it would look odd for me to dress in it. I know women usually wear something finer at their weddings, but it'll have to do. Besides, it's appropriate because it's one of the Tudor colours."

There was a brief silence, during which Mrs. Goldwell seemed to be deciding whether or not to say something. "Lady Mary, being a Tudor isn't all this is about," she began, but I stopped her.

"It is. For me, it is. And for Thomas. We've both been in agreement about it from the start." My reply sounded final enough to end any further discussion.

Although she clearly wasn't satisfied, she changed the subject. "The sergeant porter asked me to remind you to prepare a letter of intent, which should be sealed."

"I haven't forgotten. I'm going to write it now."

"So, everything is in order. Send me word if you think of anything else."

She left, and I sat down with paper and pen and sealing wax at the little table in my bedroom and wrote a simple statement that Thomas and I had been betrothed for several months and that I intended to marry him that night in his apartment at Whitehall. Finishing, I signed and dated it, then folded and sealed it and placed it in my cabinet. Then, I went to the open window and looked out at the uninteresting view, for the first time in days thinking of nothing at all.

10

At midday I saw Thomas in the Great Hall at dinner. Although we weren't able to speak with each other, merely being in his presence was reassuring. Late that afternoon I hurried through my routine trips to the kitchen and wine cellar so as to have as much time as possible with him if I found him in his apartment after finishing my errands. Luck was with me, and he was there.

His being as eager to see me as I him was made apparent by his meeting me right on the other side of the door when I opened it. "I've been waiting to hear the key turn," he said. "It feels like ages have passed since you've been here. I've missed you so!"

"And I you." Indeed, I hadn't realised how much until I'd seen him again that morning upon our return.

Then, for the first time, he bent down and lightly kissed me on the lips. I was surprised, for it felt completely natural for him to do so, and I didn't pull away. Our eyes met as he stood back up again, and I saw the kiss had been unplanned and he'd surprised himself as well. "Oh!" he said, and in response I merely smiled affectionately. I barely noticed it was the first time I'd ever been touched by a man in an intimate way. Although I still had concerns over the novelty of what was approaching on my wedding night, my conversation about it with Mrs. Goldwell had greatly put me at ease.

We went into the parlour, but were both too restless to sit, and instead stood standing in the centre. He said, "I had a small fear you'd return to tell my you'd changed your mind. But only a small one."

"You needn't have had it at all. I'm absolutely certain this is the right thing for me to do. It's as though this marriage is something life has been steering me towards. It feels as though I was guided to you that first day we talked last January."

"Yes, yes. It was like I'd been sent to wait downstairs by the Water Gate, where our paths would cross. And if I didn't know something important would come of it right then, I certainly did when you came here afterward. When I opened the door for you that day, a new chance at life seemed to stand there, waiting to enter."

"I felt the same. Then when I got to know you, I saw the person you were, and was sure of it." I stepped back from him and breathed deeply, as though to anchor myself in the present, to attend to what needed to be done. "Is everything ready?"

"Yes. I've paid the minister half his fee, but am holding the rest for him until the wedding, to be sure he's here as planned. I've also arranged for an old friend of mine to accompany him here and back. It's probably unnecessary, because he's recommended as reliable by several fellows I know. But I want to be sure. He also has a reputation for minding his own business. So do all the others who'll be here."

"Who are they?"

"My son, brother and sister. We haven't told the other children yet. We weren't going to tell my sister either but decided to, and when we did, she insisted on being present. Also, our good family friend Mr. Cawsley from Cambridge, and his friend and his wife."

"I'll have only Mrs. Goldwell with me. But I already feel as though your friends and family are mine."

"You want no one else from your family?" he asked, in a way that made me think he didn't want me to feel diminished by not having any.

"No. It's unfortunate that my sister isn't here to attend me, which of course isn't possible. But even if it were, I'm not sure I'd include her. She's not very thoughtful of what she does and says, and what might come of it. No, Mrs. Goldwell is going to be fine for me. She's quite the opposite of Catherine in so many ways."

"She's been very helpful while you've been away at Greenwich."

"She was attending my mother when she died a few years ago. My mother liked her and relied on her. Having her here is very close to my having a family member with me."

Seeing I was content, he said, "Soon you'll be counting all my family as yours."

I left a short while later, making my way back to the queen's outer room. When I arrived there, I was surprised to see new faces. A third cousin of my mother's was there with two girls who were clearly her daughters. They were members of the same branch of the royal family as the Earl of Huntington. Unlike him, the mother had retained the queen's friendship and held an important position among the gentlewomen by having charge of the queen's wardrobe, which kept her at court most of the time. Her daughters, my fourth cousins, I'd never met.

"Lady Mary! Cousin!" she called out as soon as she saw me, bringing her daughters forward. She introduced them and told me that one was fourteen and the other eleven. Instantly, I readied myself to contend with the possibility of my condition being startling to those meeting me for the first time, but it was clear at once that my young cousins had been told of it in advance and they remained perfectly poised.

Each curtsied deeply to me, and I did the same. "Very nice to meet relatives," I said, smiling at their mother, who was elegant and refined in manner and didn't ignore me as many others at court did. We were on cordial terms, and although she did nothing that could be described as friendly, she in a silent way conveyed to me a sense of shared identity in our both being part of the royal family, different from all the others. Her two daughters, resembling her with their narrow faces and small, average features, already seemed to carry the same awareness in the perfectly still way they stood on either side of her. They also both looked very frightened and alert, as though at any moment they'd be asked something they wouldn't understand. I sympathised, remembering how overwhelmed I'd been by the court on the first day I'd arrived. "One's first visit here is always a memorable occasion," I said kindly, "even though it can be unsettling."

"I hadn't expected so much chaos when we arranged the visit," their mother explained. "I'd thought it would be quieter, with everyone going to the Durham House wedding tomorrow night, and that it would be a good time for a visit before the queen's progress keeps me away for so long. I'd also thought I wouldn't be going to Durham House, or that the queen would need me in advance. But now I find that not only must I accompany her there, but she wants to wear a new dress, which is being made right now. Lady Mary, could I impose on you to be my daughters' companion while I'm not available? I can't think of anyone more appropriate. I might have asked the Countess of Lennox, but that's impossible, and what other relative have we here but the queen herself?"

"None," I said, thinking that if there were, I might not be attended at my own wedding only by Mrs. Goldwell. But my only other cousin on the royal side, Lady Margaret Strange, had birthed several children since her marriage and was away from court caring for them. Any of her children, though, would stand behind mine in the succession, and on the rare occasions when I did see her, she was courteous but aloof in the same way as the Countess of Lennox, for I could still be a competitor.

"You'll only have to keep them company here today and tomorrow while I'm inside, and introduce them to anyone who might be interested. And tomorrow night when I'm away, could I arrange a little supper for the three of you in your rooms, so you won't have to have to go to the Great Hall? It can be rather lonely there when so much of the court is absent at a celebration elsewhere. After supper, they can retire for the night back in my rooms, so it shouldn't keep you too late. Can you help me? I'd be so grateful."

Thinking rapidly, I calculated that we could be finished before nine o'clock, when I'd be expected at Thomas's apartment. I saw that the distraction might actually be helpful in maintaining my resolve, not giving me time for second thoughts. "Yes," I told her.

A look of gratitude and satisfaction appeared on her face, like a great problem had been solved. "Oh, thank you so much! I'll remember your kindness."

I looked from one daughter to the other, and saw some relaxation in the manner of each, as though they'd avoided some dreadful alternative. I said, "I'm afraid you might find me uninteresting. I'm not typical of the courtiers here." To their mother, I said, "You fit in here in ways I don't."

Before she could reply, the door to the queen's inner apartments opened, and Mrs. Parry appeared, looking about the room until she saw her. Waving, she called out, "The queen is asking for you. She won't let them do anything else to the dress until you see it!"

Everyone else in the crowded room abruptly stopped talking, turning towards us to see whose opinion the queen so valued. The two daughters seemed awestruck, but still shrank a little closer to their mother. "Thank heavens — you got here just in time!" she said to me. Turning quickly to each daughter, she went on, "I leave you in excellent company. Despite what she says, Lady Mary is proficient at everything here. I'll check on you as soon as I can." She then hurried off after Mrs. Parry.

"Come, let us sit down," I said to them, taking them to a little group of chairs at the side. As we sat, I told them I didn't want to sit too far back so that they might be able to meet anyone who looked of interest to them.

"You don't have to introduce us to anyone," the older one said quietly, without much expression. "We're only here because we wanted to spend time with our mother."

"I'm sorry, you must be disappointed. I know I must be a poor substitute."

"No, you seem very nice," the younger one answered. "And at least you're a family member. We're not the same as everybody else, you know. We're part of the royal family."

"We are," I said, as though I believed we were very fortunate and special to be so, because her tone had hinted that she'd have preferred not to be. "We should be very grateful to be who we are."

For a while, we spoke quietly, them telling me about their studies. From time to time, I would point out someone new entering the room, passing through to see the queen, but they responded with only the mildest of interest. When we ran out of things to talk about, I asked if they played any instruments, and offered to find some used by the gentlewomen. Both declined, saying that although they could play many of them, they wouldn't be comfortable doing so around so many strangers. Finally, I asked if they'd like to play a card game, and they stared at me before replying that they didn't know how. "Nobody plays cards at home," the older one said.

"I've recently learned and can show you. Let's find a quiet table in the next room, and I'll see if any of the courtiers have a deck we can use. If not, I'll go in get one of the queen's from Mrs. Parry."

Both seemed more interested in this than in anything else I'd spoken of. As we stood up, I said, "Here at court you should know how to play at least some of the games if you're here for a while — especially if you're part of the royal family."

In the next room several gentlemen were playing at different tables, and we found an empty one by a window overlooking the central garden. I approached the gentlemen to ask for a deck, and they looked amused at the request but readily obliged, making cheerful remarks about how they hoped I wouldn't lose too much money to my younger companions. Back at my own table, I sat down and began to explain the various games I'd so recently learned myself.

Later that night, I told Thomas, "They responded so eagerly. All the tension they felt about being in the palace and their disappointment over their mother's absence vanished. I enjoyed being with them."

He'd seen the girls with me in the Great Hall at supper, where they'd insisted on sitting instead of with their mother, closer to the queen. The places at my table had easily been adjusted to accommodate them. But when Thomas asked me what their names were, I couldn't remember them. I felt very shallow and insincere; when I saw them tomorrow, I would immediately have to use some subtle way to find out.

I must have looked as uncomfortable as I felt, for Thomas immediately said that it was no wonder I'd forgotten them, with so much else occupying my mind. "I've been the same," he said. "I can think of nothing else but our wedding, hoping I haven't forgotten anything." He reached into his pocket and withdrew a little cloth-wrapped object. "I've been keeping your wedding ring here for fear of losing it." When he unwrapped it, the simple gold ring glittered in the candlelight. I could scarcely believe that I would be wearing it by the same time tomorrow.

In the morning, I was able to easily learn my cousins' names without them knowing I'd forgotten them. They were at first reserved again, accompanying their mother to the prayer service and then sitting with her at breakfast, but after they joined me, they gradually became more relaxed, and even began to find amusement in the frantic hurrying about of the courtiers and gentlewomen as the departures for Durham House began. Thomas had told me a fleet of barges had been arranged for continuous trips throughout the day, for not everyone was attending all parts of the celebrations. Some courtiers were going to the morning wedding, midday banquet and afternoon entertainments, and others, including the queen, were attending later for the grander supper, tournament and masques that were to follow. Thomas's presence at the Water Gate was required all day, with a respite between late afternoon when the queen departed, and two o'clock the next morning when the return trips would begin. Although we saw each other briefly at breakfast, as expected he wasn't at midday dinner. I was grateful that by then my cousins had again taken to me sufficiently to want to sit with me, their presence keeping my thoughts occupied.

That afternoon, after the three of us had played cards again, we were entertained by a small disruption over the Durham House invitations. A very disgruntled Spanish ambassador arrived in the queen's outer room and looked around, seemingly searching for someone to bring a message further inside. Then, seeing I was the only one of the queen's attendants there, he came to me, bowed, and asked if he could speak with her regarding his intended presence at Durham House. I went inside and told Mrs. Parry, who after speaking to the queen accompanied me back to the ambassador and asked him to go to the garden, where the queen would meet him shortly.

After he did, she told me, "The French ambassador has been at Durham House for the ceremony and dinner, and was supposed to leave so the Spanish one could attend the later celebrations. But the French one has learned the queen is only expected later, and is now refusing to leave. The queen already said she wouldn't attend if both ambassadors were there at the same time, for any preference shown towards either would be seen as political, and she didn't want to contend with it. Already, the Spanish ambassador feels slighted and wants her to intervene. We'll see what she does!" She then smiled at me as though she found the incident as entertaining as I did, and hurried back inside.

A few moments later, the doors opened again and the queen, dressed in a gown she'd hurriedly put on to meet the ambassador, passed through quickly. The expression on her face revealed nothing, but the briskness of her walk told of her irritation and determination to resolve the matter. The two gentlewomen following were nearly running to keep pace with her. She passed us, and my young cousins curtsied as I did, but of course she didn't notice. When she'd vanished through the doors the ambassador had gone through, I said to them, "It'll be no time at all before she returns. She already knows exactly what she wants to say." Their interest was apparent, even though they were silent. They stayed so until, exactly like I'd said, the queen returned within minutes, a satisfied-looking Spanish ambassador at her side. Almost directly in front of us, they stopped, the ambassador bowing, then walking backwards to the corridor door, while the queen turned and went back to her inner rooms. As the two accompanying gentlewomen passed us, we heard one say quietly, "Silly little men, these ambassadors."

"And that," I told my cousins, "is how it is all the time here in the palace."

The supper their mother had arranged for us was nicely prepared and sent to my rooms at the requested time. My servants set the table, then waited in the corridor while we ate. We talked easily while we did, their informal manner remaining, but at one point I found myself thinking of the contrast with the dinner I'd had with Thomas's family, which had been livelier but also smoother. That difference ran deeper than mere manners: it was from an unusual self-awareness in my cousins' behaviour. Only once did it disappear, when right after we finished the supper, the younger of the two smiled slightly at her sister and suggested they show me what they called their 'scene.' The older one finally gave in to her entreaties, and, announcing that they were Queen Elizabeth and Mary Queen of Scots, the sisters proceeded to engage in a pretence of slapping, pushing, and pulling the hair of each other, all the while exchanging protesting remarks of ridiculous politeness. I was so startled I had no idea how to respond, and when they finished, I thanked them and went on to talk of something else. It was fortunate that no one else had been present for the display, for the queen might then hear of it, and I doubted she would appreciate having been such a source of amusement to her cousins.

When a little later I told them goodnight and sent them on their way to their mother's rooms, it was with the understanding that although they were distanced from the throne in their part of the royal family, it was still central to how they experienced life. For the first time I wondered if those with no connection to it at all — simple, ordinary people — weren't better off than we were.

But it was late, drawing near nine o'clock, not the time for me to be thinking about relatives I'd be unlikely to see again for years, after tomorrow. I went into my bedroom and took my letter of intent from the cabinet. Then I set off to meet Mrs. Goldwell, who would accompany me to Thomas's apartment. I'd decided that making my way alone through the dark corridors of the palace for such an important occasion would be lacking in some way, and I wanted the company.

It was odd to hear so much conversation from Thomas's parlour as soon as we entered it, and then to see so many people in it, all of whom turned and greeted me as though I were the queen herself. The room was less dim than it usually was when I visited at night, the result of the many candles of two extra candelabras on stands that had been brought in and whose gentle light now danced in the cool breezes from the open window. Thomas came towards me and then introduced me to his guests, each of whom I acknowledged with polite gratitude for their attendance. I wanted no misunderstanding on anyone's part that the marriage was anything other than completely intentional. When the introductions were over, I gave my sealed letter of intent to Thomas, who then passed it to his brother.

The minister was a short, squat man wearing the usual black robe and holding what I recognised was the Book of Common Prayer. "Let us begin," he said, taking his place in the centre. I stepped before him with Thomas, who was already holding the little ring he'd showed me before. More rapidly than I'd have believed possible, the minister read from the book, Thomas and I said the correct responses, and all around us was applause as the little ring was slipped on my finger and the minister gave a final blessing. He closed the book, and everyone came forward, offering congratulations. At the table, Mrs. Goldwell poured wine from several pitchers into cups that had already been set out, which she and Thomas's sister then passed about for a salute to Thomas and me. In the background, I heard Mrs. Goldwell say, "The minister should bless the marriage bed before he leaves." The little man then quickly finished his wine and, followed by the rest of us, went into the bedroom and did exactly that, while everyone crowded in the corridor, listening. When he was finished, we stepped out of his way as he left. Then Mrs. Goldwell, standing behind Thomas and me, gently pushed us into the bedroom and closed the door behind us.

The light from the corridor vanished as the door closed, but the window wasn't shuttered and let in enough moonlight for a candle to be unnecessary. The bed curtains had been drawn on both sides, so we could each undress alone, and as I took off my bonnet, stepped out of my gown, put on the nightdress Mrs. Goldwell had made me, and unpinned my hair, I could hear Thomas's movements on the other side. I finished first and pulled back the curtain, sliding in under the light blanket. I rested on the pillows which Mrs. Goldwell, as promised, had arranged exactly as I needed them to be.

Listening to Thomas behind the curtain of his side, I felt no anxiety, only a continuation of the efficiency I'd shown when meeting everyone before. Then, Thomas drew back the curtain, and the light was sufficient for me to see that he wore a long nightshirt that seemed like a soft cloud around him. He lifted the blanket and climbed in beside me, leaning over with no hesitation. "Mary," he said, and I felt the weight of him on me as his lips met mine.

Everything was the same but different from what I'd heard it would be, in a way that was impossible to describe. Like Mrs. Goldwell had said, he knew exactly what to do and went about it in a gentle manner, asking several times for reassurance that all was right with me. And when he'd finished and moved back onto his side of the bed, instead of hoping that we'd conceived a child, I was thinking instead that our intimacy had affected me in ways nothing had before.

For several moments I lay there silently, listening to his steady breathing and feeling the motion of it in the bed around me. Then, he turned towards me and said, "We should go back out to the others."

"I'd rather stay here with you," I replied.

He reached over and lightly touched my hair. "We have to. It's important for them to see that this was completed. We must remember to do everything right."

We each drew the bed curtains again when we were standing, and I made use of the basin of water and cloths that Mrs. Goldwell had left out on my side. The nightdress had stayed in position beneath me while being drawn aside at the front, and even in the dim light I could see the bloodstain that Thomas would now show the waiting guests, so there would be no question that we were man and wife. I then dressed and fixed my hair and bonnet, finishing more quickly than him. While waiting, I heard him sigh and say aloud, "It's caught on something."

I went around to his side of the bed and saw him trying to release the back of his shirt, which had become tangled. I smiled as I went and undid it. Doing so, my being so much smaller than him no longer seemed to matter, and to me we felt like equals.

"How nice to be married again," he then said, the simple remark making me feel as important as if I'd been crowned queen. It was a wonderful thing to be so appreciated for something so small.

I picked up the nightdress, then showed him how to unfold it easily so the bloodstain could be seen by the others. "I'll wait in here while you do, then bring it back and I'll come out with you." Mrs. Goldwell had already told me she'd dispose of the nightdress afterwards.

He took it and went out, and I heard more applause and congratulations, which were then repeated for me a moment later after he'd brought the nightdress back in and I'd gone out with him. More wine was poured, and we were saluted again. Then Thomas called for everyone's attention, and thanked them for having participated in so important an occasion with us. But it was time, he said, to disperse. He reminded them that for some months we wouldn't want the marriage spoken of, and he was sure he could rely on them not to.

After they'd all left, I was alone with him briefly in the parlour while Mrs. Goldwell went to the bedroom for the nightdress. Although nothing felt much different from every other time I'd been there playing cards with him at that hour, I was deeply aware that it was. "I feel I shouldn't be leaving," I told him. "I wish I could stay. But it's about the time I usually return from here, and I'd rather my servants not notice anything different." Trying for my earlier efficient manner, I continued, "Besides, we should be satisfied with what we've accomplished here tonight." But the remark sounded trivial, and it was suddenly of the utmost importance to me that he understood how I really felt. "Thomas," I began gently, not sure what words would follow. But at that moment, Mrs. Goldwell appeared in the doorway.

She saw she was interrupting us. "Your plan was to leave now," she said to me hesitantly.

"Yes, thank you. I know I have to."

"I'll wait by the door," she replied, and left to give us time alone.

"You have to go," Thomas said, then leaned forward and kissed me. A year ago it would have been difficult to believe that I would be kissed in such a way by my husband.

I stepped back from him, wanting to say something, but feeling that anything would be inadequate. Somehow, he understood, and said, "Yes, it's so difficult to find the right words, isn't it? To try to describe what this means to each of us. But there'll be time for it, in the years ahead. Tonight, we should stay with what we've decided. If we can see each other for even the smallest time tomorrow, I'll be satisfied. I'll make do with it until I see you again."

The queen was to leave with the court tomorrow, in the afternoon, for the start of her progress. I had to go with her, and so our having the second night we'd hoped for wasn't going to be possible. Suddenly, the thought of a separation from Thomas of so many weeks seemed impossible. But there was nothing that could be done.

It was time for me to leave him and return to my rooms. "Yes, I must go now. And if I do, you may be able to get some rest before the barges begin to return from Durham House."

He walked me to the apartment door, where Mrs. Goldwell was waiting. But after we said goodnight to Thomas and she and I passed through the door he opened for us, I didn't hear it close again until we'd turned the corner at the far end of the corridor. And I didn't remove my wedding ring until I was nearly back at my own rooms.

I slept soundly, and in the morning I awoke with an almost serene awareness that my life had permanently changed. The agitation and uncertainty which had been my constant background companion over the past few weeks was gone. Everything yesterday had gone perfectly. My being with child already was a possibility, although I knew it unlikely, and I wished there could be many more nights for Thomas and I to spend together, as there usually were for newly married husbands and wives. But as I lay alone in my own bed and thought of how it had been to be in Thomas's, I wasn't sure if the reason I wanted to return there was to further our plan, or to repeat the intimacy of our brief time together.

He wasn't at breakfast, but I hadn't expected him to be. I knew from the talk of the gentlewomen after prayers that although the queen had left Durham House when planned, it had been near dawn before all barges had returned. Neither the queen nor many of the courtiers had been at prayers, and they weren't at breakfast, everyone knowing that she typically slept late after such events, and they wouldn't be missed if they did the same. I saw my young cousins again at both, and said goodbye to them since they were to leave immediately afterward. Doing so, I was unable to prevent myself from smiling when I thought of their silly enactment of a battle between queens Elizabeth and Mary. Hopefully I would remember to one day describe it for Thomas. His children, too, undoubtably displayed such mirth from time to time, and I looked forward to the days when I would be there to see it in the Lewisham household.

During the morning, everything quickly became very chaotic with much rushing about as more and more courtiers appeared and attended to the departure from the palace, which wouldn't be returned to until the autumn. Corridors were crammed with servants carrying trunks, many more than for the previous shorter trip to Greenwich. A few went to the Water Gate but mostly to the others used for the commerce, to be loaded either on barges or wagons in the seemingly endless procession that followed the court on its journeys. It was Thomas's responsibility to supervise all of it, and I knew I couldn't get in his way on so busy a day. Yet it was of the utmost importance for us to see each other again before I left, even for a moment. After attending to my own trunk and the closing of my rooms, I went to the queen's to see if I was needed. If not, I would ask Mrs. Parry if I could be absent for a while, since I could no longer use the excuse of my daily trip to the wine cellar and kitchen.

I found her standing in the midst of several open trunks, directing the gentlewomen and servants packing them. She looked at me as I reached her, but it was clear her thoughts were mostly on her task.

"I'd like to go and say goodbye to a friend who's staying here, if I can?" I requested.

"Yes, of course." Very briefly, she smiled, a touch of interest flitting across her face as she focused on me. "How nice you have friends."

"It is."

"Take your time," she said, and I hurried away.

Thomas was in the Water Gate waiting gallery, standing by the window in almost exactly the same place he'd been that day in January when things between us had begun. But instead of being alone, he was talking in a lively way to a group of porters and bargemen, gesturing back and forth out onto the river as he spoke. Seeing me approaching, he finished and dismissed them, telling them the time they were to be there later. Leaving him, they all bowed silently as they went by me.

A clerk in the office must have been waiting for his own turn to speak, for as they passed the office door he appeared, carrying a long list and saying, "Sergeant Porter, I —"

Thomas stopped him, calling, "Give me a minute. This is one of the queen's gentlewomen." The man bowed as the others had, and retreated.

"I'm so sorry to disturb you," I said as I reached him, "but I had to see you before I left!"

His face, which had first looked pleased at my appearance, showed concern. "Is something wrong?"

"No, nothing at all. Everything couldn't be more right! It's only that I didn't want to leave today without seeing you, and I thought you might not be here later. And even if you are, I'm sure we won't be able to talk together. If anything's wrong, it's that I have to go with the queen instead of staying here."

"I'm going to miss you. I'll count each day until you return."

"I, also. And when I miss you the most, I already know what I'm going to do. I'll take out my engagement and wedding rings and look at them, perhaps wear them. But I regret you not having rings of your own."

"I have this," he said, pointing to the floor beneath him. "Right here is where I stood when we first met. I have that

163

memory, and so many others, of all our card games in my apartment, and the puppy you brought me from Lord Darnley, and the wonderful day we had with my family. When I miss you, I'll take those memories out and look at them."

"Yes, yes! I can do that too. How well spent our time has been these past months, to have so many memories!"

Behind me, I heard people entering the waiting gallery on the other side, one of whom immediately called out, "Sergeant Porter!" Turning, I saw a little crowd coming towards him, while at the same time the man in the office looked out from the office door, eager not to lose his place. More than ever before, the importance of what Thomas did at the palace was clear to me. He was centrally involved in all that unfolded within it. I couldn't take any more of his time when he had so much to do.

I turned back to him. "Visit your family while I'm away. Give my best to them."

"Our family," he said. "You must think of them that way now."

Behind him, outside the window on the river, I could see several barges already beginning to assemble. I'd done what I'd wanted to, and it was time for me to leave him to his work.

I didn't say goodbye, hoping that we might see each other again when I left later, and I didn't turn around and look back as I crossed the waiting area. But when he wasn't there that afternoon when I arrived again with the queen and her attendants, I wished that I had.

"What are you looking for, Lady Mary?" Mrs. Parry asked. She was seated beside me in the barge as it pulled away from the steps, and she saw me continuing to look back at them. "You were able to say goodbye to your friend before, weren't you?"

"Yes, thank you." I couldn't explain that I'd been hoping that Thomas might appear on the steps. Instead, I said, "I like the Water Gate. It's so much a part of everything that happens in the palace."

Although it was a vague answer, it was sufficient for her, and she smiled as she looked at the gate. "Important things happen at it," she agreed pleasantly.

11

It was little more than a month later, at Windsor Castle, when a very thoughtful and more serious than usual Mrs. Parry asked me about the friend I'd mentioned the day we'd left Whitehall Palace. "It wouldn't by any chance have been Mr. Keyes, the sergeant porter, would it?"

I felt myself tense, but maintained my composure. Although I'd been hoping I wouldn't hear any such question about Thomas, I'd been preparing myself for it. The previous day I'd twice noticed little groups of courtiers turning to look quickly at me with snidely interested, amused expressions. Now, with Mrs. Parry's question, I knew my marriage had been learned of. And I also knew that if the courtiers were gossiping about it, it wouldn't be long before the queen and her councillors would know of it too.

There was no point in trying to deny it. "Yes," I replied, attempting indifference.

We were in the castle courtyard outside St. George's chapel, where we'd just been for morning prayers. Ahead of us, the queen had swiftly turned a corner and was out of view, and everyone following had shifted to a slower, more rambling pace. Only when Mrs. Parry had asked her question had I realised she'd stayed at the back, where she could speak to me alone.

Beside me, she stopped walking, but whether from surprise or to let the others get even further ahead of us, I didn't know. But as we turned to each other, I saw from the confused look on her face that she'd expected my answer to be different. And when she then slowly but pointedly asked me how good a friend he was, I could hear a tiny note of fear in her voice.

It was troubling to see Mrs. Parry, usually calm and steady, looking so worried. I had no wish to disturb her further. I sighed and asked, "Must I tell you?"

"I think so."

"I'm his wife."

Her eyes widened as she gasped and dropped her prayerbook. Since she was too startled to say anything, I continued, "We were married on the night of the wedding at Durham House. But we'd been planning it for some time."

"Does the queen know of it?" she was finally able to ask.

"Oh, no. No one besides those who attended our wedding were told of it. Certainly not the queen." Ahead of us, everyone else had rounded the same corner the queen had turned, and the courtyard seemed very vast and empty. As I looked around at the castle's strong and sturdy walls, I thought that I had as much right to be in it as the queen did — or even more, according to some. Politics and fate were the reasons why she sat on the throne instead of me, or Catherine, or the Countess of Lennox, or Lord Darnley, or perhaps because she played the game of power with such skill. Now, none of it mattered. She should know that I didn't fear her, and had taken the steps to live my life the way I wanted to.

"People here are talking about it," Mrs. Parry finally said.

"I know. Yesterday I saw several courtiers looking at me in an unusual way." The prayer book was still on the pavement where she'd dropped it, and I now bent and retrieved it.

"Thank you," she said distantly as I gave it to her, her thoughts clearly whirling.

Seeking to reassure her, I began gently, "Mrs. Parry, please, don't be so troubled. I —"

Before I could finish, she reached out and seized my sleeve. "You must tell the queen at once," she said, her voice low but insistent, "and hope that she hasn't heard it yet! Things will be more favourable for you then, if that's possible. She never likes being the last to know something."

"Yes," I agreed. "I see you are right. Is she breakfasting in the hall with the others, or in her rooms?"

"In her rooms."

"I'll go right now." It was best for me not to wait.

Mrs. Parry's expression changed to one of surprise, but this time she seemed to recognise something new in me. Still holding my sleeve, she said, "No. Let me tell her. That way, she'll have time to think it over before she decides how to respond. I know her. I've seen this before — well, not this exactly — but you need to avoid backing her into a corner. Her initial response is going to be anger, and she may feel that she cannot retreat from it later."

I was hesitant to have Mrs. Parry drawn into the matter. She had her own position to maintain with the queen, who played different versions of her game with everyone. "I can't let you —"

"Yes, you can. But oh, Lady Mary, this isn't the best time for this! She's been in such a poor mood since the news from Scotland. And this is so like it! The timing is unfortunate!" For emphasis, she tugged on my sleeve.

Three weeks earlier Mary Stuart and Lord Darnley had married. Despite the distinct possibility of it having been what the queen had secretly sought all along, her anger had been seen by everyone, suggesting that although she'd achieved what she'd wanted to, she was ambivalent because she'd been disobeyed and ignored. And at one point, as I'd watched her the day after the news had been received, I'd wondered if that marriage was making her feel suddenly alone in her unmarried state. Learning of mine now might do the same.

Mary Stuart had her new husband proclaimed king, and although the Scottish Parliament never approved the title, many had begun to regard him so, both there and abroad. Almost immediately there had been requests for the release from the Tower of the Countess of Lennox, and there was talk among the courtiers that the hopes of the Catholics were renewed that the young couple or their children might eventually take the English throne, combining both countries into one. Even now, weeks later, numerous ambassadors were arriving at Windsor to discuss the matter with the queen. Again, there was talk that she should have children of her own.

Mrs. Parry finally released my sleeve as she stepped back, drew a deep breath, and adjusted her bonnet. She was over the initial surprise and had steadied herself. Eyeing me keenly, she said, "No one would have believed this of you — although I suppose the unknown should be expected." Resolutely, she drew another breath and stood very straight. "I'll go right now."

"What a friend you've always been."

"I've tried and I'll continue to, but you've taken a difficult path. You should go to the hall for breakfast, then return to your room. I'll meet you there — if the queen lets me. Don't even think about entering her rooms until I've told you how things went."

Without speaking further, we went inside, she to the queen's rooms and me to the Great Hall where the court dined.

Windsor Castle was smaller than Whitehall Palace, and none of the courtiers liked staying there, but since the queen did, everyone knew they had to make the best of it and adjust to the cramped and uncomfortable quarters. Tables and benches were very close together in the crowded Great Hall and adjacent rooms needed to accommodate everyone. Since I'd come in late there was barely space, despite my small size, for me to fit in my assigned place and eat some of the cold beef and bread being served. I usually wasn't hungry at breakfast and ate little, but today I took a substantial amount to fortify myself for what would be a difficult time ahead. Thoughts of the conversation happening between Mrs. Parry and the queen caused me to feel touches of apprehension, but I was able to hold them off. When I from time to time looked around at the other tables, not once did I see anyone looking at me, which I decided was a hopeful sign.

The rooms for the gentlewomen and other courtiers were fewer at the castle than at any of the palaces. Although I didn't have to share mine, it was tiny, with barely enough space for my serving woman to every night set out her pallet on the floor, and her husband, his, in the corridor outside my door, where the couple usually passed most of the day. The first sign that things hadn't gone the best way possible was that neither of them was there when I returned after breakfast.

Inside the room, I found Mrs. Parry, standing and staring at the door as it opened. She looked like she'd just been in a battle instead of an encounter with the queen.

"It went poorly," I said, sparing her the difficulty of how to begin.

"Worse than I thought it would," she said, as though still surprised by it. "She actually screamed and threw things. It was only with effort that I convinced her to let me be the one to tell you you're to stay in your room until you're told otherwise. Your servants have already been taken away. You're not to speak with anyone except me without permission. I've assumed responsibility for you, for now." She stared at me meaningfully. "So don't make a fool out of me, Lady Mary."

"Never."

"The most important thing she wants to know is if the marriage was completed, and if so, if a child is expected."

"It was completed but there is no child. I had my flow as usual a week ago."

"Thank goodness for that! It would have made things so much more complicated, as it did for Catherine. I doubt it'll go as badly for you now, as for her. There are going to be doctors' examinations, likely very soon. But if it's as you say, much trouble has been avoided. Even so, it's not going to be easy to get past this. I tried my best to reassure the queen that you're a poor little thing who didn't understand what she was doing, but so far, I don't think she's accepted it. It's going to take a while to convince her."

Her words about my being a poor little thing seemed to echo around me. Of course, Mrs. Parry's intention had only been to be helpful, but she had thoroughly diminished who I was. No matter what she, the queen, or anyone else thought, it was time for them to learn differently about me.

"I knew exactly what I was doing," I said quietly. "I decided I wanted to marry and then found the best husband I could. It wasn't a mistake. I don't regret it."

"Yes, but if you appear to —"

"I'm not the poor little thing you described!"

"Oh, my dear, I know you're not! But wouldn't it be best for the queen to think that?"

"No."

"Perhaps the marriage can be undone," she said. "It's the best solution. Everything then would stay the same —"

171

I stopped her by suddenly laughing aloud. "For me to remain the same Crouchback Mary, drifting through life in the corners of the queen's palaces? No." I went to the trunk at the end of my bed, opened it and found the little case where I'd put the rings Thomas had given me. Taking them out, I slipped them on, then turned back to Mrs. Parry. "See?" I said, showing her the fingers they were on. "The sergeant porter — my husband Thomas — gave me these when we became engaged a few months ago, and this is my wedding ring. I'm his wife now. The marriage took place in his apartment on the night of the wedding at Durham House, and the ceremony was conducted by a proper minister and attended by many people. We made great efforts to make sure it couldn't be undone! And even if it could, I wouldn't want it to be."

At first, Mrs. Parry said nothing, arranging her thoughts. Then, she said in a very gentle and almost pleading way, "Lady Mary, is it possible you haven't been seeing all of this correctly? I know the sergeant porter isn't a young and foolish fellow, and is known for his reliability. But the queen has already said that she's inclined to hold him more responsible for this, and that he led you into it. Are you sure that isn't how it is — that you haven't been deluded by him? If you were, it can go better for you, at least. I think that's what the queen wants you to claim. If you do, I'm sure she can find a way to have the marriage undone."

But the thought that I would even consider blaming Thomas was completely unacceptable to me. "No! I'll not even hear that suggested! I could never treat him so. We decided this together. I knew fully what I was doing, and I'll never say otherwise."

"Lady Mary," Mrs. Parry said very directly, "the queen fears you. And she won't accept you not fearing her in return."

"I know that. And it's not only the fear of my being used politically. I reflect a part of her that she fears one day might wish to do the same. And so she's going to try her best to undo my marriage, to reassure herself she'll never do what I did. But it's impossible for me to be other than I now am."

Mrs. Parry was listening to me with deep interest, as though I were telling a tale completely new to her. She herself had never married, and in the silent moment that followed I wondered why. My not knowing seemed to suggest some failure in me as a friend, since I'd never shown enough interest to find out. Lately I'd noticed that I'd been distant in other ways, often not remembering the names of those around me, like my servants and young cousins. My bond with Thomas now showed me how vaguely I'd been passing through life.

"I can't go back to how I was," I told Mrs. Parry. "I can't."

"Are you in love with him?" she asked, trying to understand.

"I don't know. I'm not certain what that's supposed to feel like. I know it's not the way Catherine was with Edward Seymour. We like and respect each other, and I think love could follow later. I've seen him put my interests ahead of his, and he's seen me do the same. What more could we ask for as a sign of future contentment with each other? We married because we saw it would suit both of us to do so."

"Are you absolutely certain no one encouraged either of you in this? Especially anyone with Catholic or Reformed sympathies?"

"No one did. Neither of us feels strongly enough about religion one way or the other. We were married according to the Anglican practice the queen wants us all to follow."

"That should help. I'll tell the queen that." She leaned back against the door for a moment's rest, now that she knew what her next steps would be. "I have to go back to her now; she's expecting me. She won't like hearing that you're not the silly creature she thinks you. But it's going to help that there's no child she'd have to contend with, and that there's no politics involved."

"Should I accompany you this time? You shouldn't have to do this alone."

She looked at me strangely. "Alone," she said. "I've been alone all my life." And I knew then that if anyone could convince the queen, she could. No matter what advice she was giving me, she sympathised with what I'd done.

"Stay here," she said. "I'll know better what to tell you when I see what mood the queen is in, now that she's had time to think. But it's best if you do nothing until then."

As she was opening the door, I remembered my servants, who'd spent so much time sitting outside it. I asked if she knew where they were, and my concerns receded when she said they'd been moved to stay with the queen's servants, but had not been told why.

"Please tell the queen neither knows anything about this. Nothing at all."

She went out, and the little room suddenly felt as empty as the outdoor courtyard had earlier. I looked down at my rings, the way I'd told Thomas I would when I missed him, which I suddenly did very much. Very soon, he would find out what had happened. If I could have one wish granted, it would be for me to be with him when he did.

12

The house on Minories Street wasn't far outside London's Aldgate, and as the cart I'd hired to sit in amidst my few belongings — no expensive coach for me — passed through the gate, the significance of it wasn't lost upon me. It'd been at another such gate, the Water Gate, when the most important changes in my life had begun. For my new home to be so situated seemed relevant, but in what way, I wouldn't speculate about. Certainly, the changes that'd taken place years before hadn't been what I'd expected.

There were only a few days left in September, but the weather was still mild and pleasant. At midday, as the cart pulled up to the two-storey timber and plaster-fronted house, I saw one lower window and two on the second floor were open for airing, no doubt the work of Mrs. Parry. As promised, she was waiting for me just outside the front door.

In the seven years since I'd last seen her on that day when she'd brought the news of my marriage to the furious queen, she looked not to have aged at all. During all the time that had followed, when I'd been banished from court and lived with a succession of custodians who'd ranged from resentful to kindly, I'd been allowed no contact with her. By the time the queen had finally relented and decided I could reside on my own, I'd had no idea if my old friend was even still in the world of the living. It had been a good day indeed when directly on the heels of the queen's decision I'd heard from her, with an offer to help me obtain a house, making use of the new pension the queen was granting me. The amount was more than satisfactory, a sign of my once again being in favour.

The only condition was that I never attempted to marry again; the validity of my marriage had never been acknowledged by her, though she had never managed to undo it. Only Thomas's death had succeeded in ending it.

Thomas had died a year ago. He'd fared both worse and better than me, having been first confined in London's Fleet Prison for two years. But he'd then been released and allowed to return to his home in Lewisham, and was eventually for the second time made Captain of Sandgate Castle. The queen always sought to make use of whoever she could, and she had known his talents were useful. I'd been told as much, and no more. I had no idea if, like me, he'd continued to hope for the day when we'd be able to live together, or if instead he'd regretted ever having met me.

On the street a little way from the front of the house was an unmoving coach of the type the queen had been starting to use when I'd still been attending her, with the driver and two footmen in the queen's livery standing next to it. As Mrs. Parry, who must have arrived in it, came forward to the cart, she motioned for them to assist me from it, quickly ordering them to take my trunk and other bags into the house. Although I didn't require assistance, she then herself helped me from the cart, saying, "Not a fit way for a cousin of the queen to travel. A coach, or at least a horse should have been sent."

We then embraced, and she stepped back and looked at me. "Not so bad as I'd thought," she said. "Not bad at all. You don't even look much older."

"I'm twenty-seven. My custodians always saw that I had the best of care, wherever I was. Even when they resented my presence, they knew they were answerable to the queen." There was no need to mention that I knew my condition hadn't progressed in any noticeable way either. I'd been allowed exercise on the grounds and in the gardens of the different mansions where I'd stayed. One of the doctors who'd attended me during that time had mentioned that walking could help my condition, and I now looked forward to doing more of it. My new house being where it was would give me access to the fields and open roadways of the suburbs, and I intended to make use of them.

Mrs. Parry said, "I didn't know how comfortable you would be with stairs, so I found a property with a room on the ground floor that can be a bedroom, if you wish. But I couldn't find any with access to the back yard from the front, for a horse to be kept back there. So, if you want one, you'll have to keep it at a stable. There's one down the street."

"Stairs are fine. I haven't been riding in years and don't have plans to now. Perhaps eventually I'd want horses for a coach of my own. But I first have to see how my expenses are, and if I can afford the price of hay and a stable."

"You'll find out."

"I've never kept a house before."

"That's why I sought a small one. At first, I thought that your establishment should reflect who you are to the queen. But then I decided that was less important than finding a place you'd be comfortable in."

"Thank you. Yes, that's the important thing." The house I was standing in front of looked as though it would suit me perfectly; it was neat and compact, like all the others on Minories Street. The fact that it was attached to those on either side seemed to connect it to everyday life, which I myself now looked forward to being part of.

The footmen and coachman returned from bringing my belongings inside. Through the first-floor window, I saw someone within pass by. "I've hired two servants for you to start with," Mrs. Parry explained. "I did seek out Mrs. Goldwell, as you asked, but unfortunately she passed away a few years ago. But a nephew of hers and his wife were available. I liked them, and I thought you would too. Come, let's go in and meet them, and see what you think of your new home." Turning to the men with the coach, she tossed them some coins and told them to find a nearby tavern for dinner. "We'll sit and talk for some time," she went on as she showed me inside. "So many things have happened that I doubt you've been told of."

The two servants, in their twenties, met us right inside the Front door, where the man bowed and his wife curtsied. I offered them condolences on the death of his aunt. It was clear they'd been told of my condition, for neither looked at me in a surprised way. Henry and Anne Goldwell were their names, which I resolved to use not only when addressing them, but in my thoughts. Both had dark hair, but while Henry's eyes were blue, Anne's were a deep and thoughtful brown.

Henry said, "It's an honour to serve you. Aunt Frances always told me you were a great lady."

"That she is," Mrs. Parry agreed. I thanked him, although it had been startling to hear him say so. Only once before had anyone said that about me, and that had been Thomas. But I didn't know if by the end he'd still thought so.

I'd expected the parlour to be unfurnished, but it was full of good tables, chairs, benches and cabinets. "It's all yours," Mrs. Parry told me. "I bought it outright, even though the house is being leased. The previous tenants moved to the Continent and left almost everything. They were Catholics who went to Spain when things became more difficult for them here, after the Pope excommunicated the queen. I don't think you would have heard about that, though."

"I didn't. I was told little of anything, especially politics. I suppose Catherine's death was something my custodians felt they had to let me know about, since she was my sister. Even so, my request to attend her funeral was refused." I'd grieved for Catherine, but her death at the age of twenty-seven — the same age I was now — hadn't surprised me. The last news I'd heard of her before I'd been sent from court had been of her increased despondency, and among the few things I'd been allowed to know after she'd died was that she'd begun to sicken physically not long after that, when she'd understood there'd be no change in her circumstances anytime soon. Her natural disposition hadn't been a solitary one, and the despair of the long, tedious hours had been unrelieved even by the presence of the younger son she'd been allowed to keep with her. Despite the ministrations of excellent doctors sent by the queen, she'd wasted away and died nearly five years ago.

I looked at Mrs. Parry questioningly. "I still don't know what became of the earl, or their sons."

"Catherine's death improved things for the earl. He's back at court sometimes now. The boys are living with his mother, but their parents' marriage is still unrecognised by the queen and Parliament, so they've no place in the succession. But we'll speak more of your family later; for now, let's finish showing you the house."

I followed her, looking at everything she showed me with a new appreciation of small, everyday things. Behind the parlour was a windowless dining room, sufficient for the table in its centre and a sideboard. Mrs. Parry opened the sideboard doors, showing me the plates and platters within. "Not silver, but eventually you'll have some for when you have guests."

The kitchen also had cupboards full of utensils, plates and pans, which Anne Goldwell was pleased to show me. There was also the aroma of food in the air, from the pot on the stove with the pottage she'd prepared for midday dinner. "I'm not much of a cook yet," she told me shyly. "But I'll do my best. You must let me know what your favourite dishes are and I'll have them for you." There were windows and a door in the back kitchen wall, opening into a deep, enclosed yard that was the width of the house. From the window I could see the remnants of a garden, with a shed at the rear.

Next to the kitchen was the small room Mrs. Parry had said could be a bedroom. It had a good bed and other furniture, as did the other bedrooms upstairs. Mrs. Parry told me that all of the mattresses, blankets, bedcurtains, covers, and household linens had been newly purchased. Even so, when I went to one of the bedroom cabinets and opened it, I half expected to find the clothes of the previous owners still in it. But they were empty, as the entire house had been, waiting for a new beginning.

Back downstairs in the parlour, Mrs. Parry asked, "Is everything to your liking?"

"It's perfect. You've done an excellent job, like you always do. It's why the queen finds you indispensable."

"Everyone, my dear, can be replaced. The ones who forget it usually are. The queen especially knows it."

Behind the dining room the door to the kitchen opened, and Henry asked if we were ready to dine. We told him yes and took our places at the table, which he'd already set for us. Doing so, I could scarcely believe it was mine, like everything else around me.

"I wonder about the people who moved from here," I said. "I hope that in Spain they've settled into another comfortable new home. It's strange to think that all this was left here because of religion. Either the Catholic or Reformed faith would be fine for me. I've read many books about them lately — there wasn't much more to do most of the time — and I still find one is as good as the other."

"Be sure not to speak of that when you visit the queen," Mrs. Parry warned. "Last month, something terrible began in France — a massacre of the Reformed by the Catholics. It's not even known if it's over yet; it started in Paris and spread to other cities. Thousands have been killed already. The queen had all the courtiers dress in black along with her when she received the French ambassador to hear his explanation of what had happened, which he couldn't fully provide. Many of the French have arrived at our ports, and the queen has welcomed them. She's aware that it's possible that the same thing could happen here, either identically or in reverse — especially with an alternative Catholic queen available, Mary Stuart. So you mustn't let any of the courtiers know what you think about Catholics in any way."

"I won't. But it's a sorry thing that everyone can't live in peace with each other."

Before she could reply, the door opened and Henry brought in a tray with the pottage, bread, and wine. As soon as he'd left, Mrs. Parry said, "I've things to tell you about your relatives, but let's enjoy our food before I do. Your first dinner in your new home!"

When we were finished, and the tableware had been cleared away, we remained where we sat. "You mentioned the idea of my visiting the queen," I said. "I suppose I must, to let her know how grateful I am to be in favour again."

"Yes, at least one visit, not too long from now. And then in the new year, she'll do the exchange of gifts with you. I'll let you know what type of gift to get her. You can give money or a silver dish, but what she really likes are things that are different, that she didn't expect. It's one of the few things one can do for her and be certain she'll appreciate it." She shifted in her chair, pulling it closer to the table. "Now, about your family. Scotland is ruled by a little king, six-year-old James Stuart. He is the son of Lord Darnley and Mary Stuart."

For an instant, time seemed to stand still around us, because of the significance of the news. My cousins in Scotland had done what I couldn't, and had a male child who could one day succeed to Elizabeth's throne. But my response was one of acceptance; I felt only a touch of regret over my own ambition, which hadn't been realised. And as I stared at Mrs. Parry, I saw the story she had to tell me was far from over. "You say he is king there," I said slowly. "For how long has he ruled?"

"Since 1567. He was crowned when he was one year old."

"What happed to his mother?"

"Mary Queen of Scots abdicated amidst widespread belief that she had been involved in the murder of Lord Darnley."

I looked away from her, at the empty table between us, wondering if she'd really said what she had. It seemed unbelievable that such a thing could have happened. And yet, there'd always been such stories of the ruthlessness of Mary Stuart, of her having murdered her first husband and destroying others for various reasons.

"Her marriage with Lord Darnley," Mrs. Parry continued, "was a disaster nearly from the beginning. Once the child was born, it seems she felt she had what she wanted in order to reinforce her claim to the English throne. Lord Darnley was killed during an explosion of the house he was staying in, shortly after Mary left. What made it all worse was that not long after, she married the man widely believed to have actually done it, Lord Bothwell. A terrible decision for her! There was a revolt and she was forced to abdicate, after which Bothwell fled to Denmark while she came into this country, to seek Elizabeth's help in regaining her throne. She's still here, in the custody of the Earl of Shrewsbury, in much the same situation you were in for so many years. But hers is worse, because she's believed to be the murderess of the queen's cousin, one who had his own claim to the throne. At first, Elizabeth seemed inclined to send her back to Scotland, but no more. And religion has become a part of it. There have been Catholic plots to remove her from custody and take her to Europe, or even to make her queen here instead of Elizabeth."

The news was almost beyond comprehension. "What of Lord Darnley's parents? His mother must have been released from the Tower by now."

"She was released almost immediately. Understandably, she was devastated by what happened. She and the earl were insistent that Mary was to blame, and they wanted Elizabeth to take action against her. When Mary abdicated, Elizabeth negotiated with the Scottish lords for the earl to return as regent, and the countess resumed her place as one of the queen's companions. So, they never achieved their ambition of becoming a king and queen themselves, but a regency was close to it, and there was the satisfaction of knowing their grandson would one day be king of Scotland in his own right. But the tragedy continued when a few years later, the earl was assassinated by one of Mary's supporters."

"The poor countess! How has she been after that?"

"Of course, it was difficult for her. She and the earl actually seemed to have loved each other — so unusual for marriages that are political! But she is who she is, and she's continued. She still has an unmarried son, and, even after everything that happened to the older one, and her now having a grandson on the Scottish throne, she's still ambitious and wants the best marriage she can find for him."

It was all so complicated to think about. Mrs. Parry sat quietly at the table while I went to the parlour's open front window and stood there, not knowing what to say. Then, she joined me at it, both of us looking out to where her coach waited. "It's easier getting around in the coach now that I'm older," she said. "I'll speak to the queen about arranging for you to have one. She'll understand. Even without my asking, she had this one waiting for me when I arrived in the city this morning. I've several other matters to attend to for her here before going back to Windsor. We'll be there for at least a month, so when you visit, you'll have to make the trip. But don't wait too long, because she's expecting it."

"How is she?" I asked, although I hadn't been sure I'd wanted to.

Mrs. Parry waited a long moment before replying, "Almost an impossible question, that. Who knows how she is? Does anyone? She's mysterious to all of us, even the ones who know her best. The most difficult thing is trying to understand whether she wants to marry or remain single. She still plays the marriage game with different suitors, and they still have hopes. Who could blame them, with a chance of becoming father to a king? She knows it, and is going to allow it for as long as time allows her to. She does have time left, although next year she'll be forty. But now the son of Mary Stuart and Lord Darnley has changed things, somewhat. His claim to the English throne is a good one, for despite being Scottish by birth his father was born here, and that could counteract our dislike of foreigners in this country. And he's being brought up in the Reformed religion. His position is different from his mother's. Already, he seems more likely to succeed Elizabeth than she does. One can only wonder if Mary Stuart's ambition is for him rather than herself now."

"That's why I married Thomas," I said. "I wanted a child who could take my place in the succession and become king. That was my reason, at first. But I now believe that even before we married, it began to be because of something different. Things changed."

"Everything changes in life. Even things that look like they've stayed the same have changed."

I turned from the window to look directly at her. "Have you heard anything of Thomas's final year?"

"Nothing. No one is interested in him anymore. His second appointment at Sandgate Castle and even his death last year was barely commented on by anyone."

I didn't know if I'd been hoping she would know more, or not. But I saw she wouldn't be able to provide any information at all.

"His family is likely still at Lewisham, you know," she offered. "I'm sure the queen wouldn't mind if you asked them."

When I didn't reply, and instead turned away from the window and asked about something in the house, she said nothing further about it.

She stayed a little while longer, then left. When she did, I walked her outside, and stood and watched as the coach drove away down Minories Street and out of view. Then I went back inside the little house.

13

It was a month later that I arrived at Windsor Castle's front gate. There, I gave the driver of the castle's provision wagon the coin I'd promised him at the town's Thames dock and got out, instead of continuing through to the household section. I wanted to walk for a while outside to steady myself before seeing the queen. As I went through the first courtyard beside St. George's Chapel, I didn't allow myself to think of the last time I'd been there, but instead I considered what lay ahead. There was no reason for me to be anything other than welcomed by the queen, and I was mostly confident I'd be received as I expected. But I wouldn't be sure until I was crossing the courtyard again in the opposite direction.

The late October day was clear but cool, and I pulled my hooded cloak closer around me. It was new, of good wool and neatly sewn, as was the brown velvet and green trimmed dress with the matching bonnet I'd had made for the occasion. My new pension from the queen allowed for occasional luxuries, and I'd decided that since she was responsible for it, it would be appropriate for me to look my best when appearing before her. But even so, I'd chosen fabrics that were quiet in colour and simple in design, reflecting who I felt myself to be.

Entering the second courtyard, I saw there were fewer people in it than in the first one, which had been busy with various vehicles. I briefly stopped and stood looking at the door to the part of the castle I was about to enter, feeling that what took place inside it no longer had anything to do with my life. I would visit the queen and then leave, returning to my house on Minories Street, which I already so valued and liked.

It took but a few minutes for me to make my way inside and to the range of rooms the queen occupied, where in the corridor I told the presiding steward I had an audience with her. "Lady Mary Grey," I said when he asked who I was, the name the queen still wanted me called by. He went inside, and a moment later returned with Mrs. Parry.

"Right on time!" she said. "And the best day for you to have chosen; everything's quiet with the queen today."

"She knows I'm expected?" She didn't like surprises, and I wanted nothing to disturb the smoothness of the meeting. "If not, maybe you should tell her I'm here?"

"I told her just now that I was about to bring you in. And she'd already been told earlier, when we went over who would be here today. She didn't comment, which was a good sign. She knows you're here to thank her for the pension, and for everyone else to see that you're in favour. It should go well!" She helped me off with my cloak, which she gave to a servant. "A pretty dress," she then commented, as she led me inside.

The outer room was crowded, full of courtiers and other visitors waiting to see the queen, and several gentlewomen dressed in green livery. On one side, in the centre of a little group was the Countess of Lennox, standing beside a young man. It took me a second to realise that he was her son, Charles. Although she appeared much the same as she had the last time that I'd seen them together at Whitehall Palace, he was very different, now about fifteen, with a look of dignity and responsibility about him. Although the countess was dressed in black, a statement of continuing mourning for the loss of her older son and her husband, Charles was not, and wore a likely expensive outfit and hat of dark green. "Is Charles Stuart Earl of Lennox now?" I asked Mrs. Parry.

"Yes, he was given the title after his father died, and the countess petitioned the queen and Parliament for it. Since Lord Darnley was dead as well, it might have gone to his son, but the countess is playing more than one game for her family. It would be quite an accomplishment for her grandson to end up on the thrones of both England and Scotland, but there's no certainty to that, and everyone's sure the countess is seeking an alternate path to the English throne in case it doesn't work out. Charles's claim is a strong one; his nephew's is a generation behind his. And he's mild in manner, which many here find appealing. He's also had a Reformed education, because although it's almost entirely Catholics in their circle, she wanted him to appeal to both sides of the religious divide. Today, they're all Catholics in that little group around them over there. But who knows how things might go politically a few years down the road?"

Charles was fair-haired and blue-eyed, and if not handsome, at least nice enough in appearance, but without the sense of determination that was still in his mother's manner as she spoke to those gathered around them. I wondered what he thought about the possibility of his becoming king one day, or if, given the sorry end of his brother Lord Darnley, it was something he wanted at all. Turning away, and walking beside Mrs. Parry towards the door to where the queen was, the thought that it could have been me standing beside a son who could be king flitted through my mind.

Nearer the door, we stopped, and Mrs. Parry said, "Let's take a moment to arrange ourselves before going in. Although I must say, you don't look like you need it."

A short distance behind her, my cousin the Earl of Huntington was standing with some gentlemen, speaking to them the same way the Countess of Lennox was to those around her, but in a more serious manner. I hadn't expected him, for the last time I'd seen him visit the queen the interview hadn't gone as he'd wanted. I asked Mrs. Parry if he was now in favour.

"I should say so!" she answered. "The queen has found him very helpful in dealing with Mary Stuart, especially since like her he has a claim to the throne, but is so completely a Reformer. He's been appointed President of the Council of the North, which shows the extent to which the queen is now ready to rely on him. Since Mary Stuart arrived here, he's been outspoken about how he despises her. It doesn't matter that they're cousins. There have been stories that she feels the same way about him."

The earl was dressed in the same way he'd been when I'd seen him last, in the dark and simple clothing of the Reformers. But there was a new confidence about him that hadn't been present back then, and he spoke to his companions with focused sincerity, the way he no doubt now maintained his position. Having been placed by the queen in the difficult political game revolving around Mary Stuart, he would be intent on fulfilling the task that had been set for him, and clearly knew that diligence would be required at all times.

"Are you ready?" Mrs. Parry asked.

"Yes." We went inside, leaving my three cousins behind, like figures on a chessboard. In the end, all their moves would be decided by the queen.

There were several courtiers surrounding the queen and speaking with her as she sat in a throne-like chair all the way on the other side of the room from where we entered. Although she must have been aware of us approaching, she continued her conversation without looking at us, which I was thankful for in that it allowed my feeling of ease to continue.

Only when I was directly in front of her and about to curtsey did she look at me. "You don't have to do that," she said, stopping the curtsey. The others around her stepped back, as did Mrs. Parry, but not before I sensed their silent acknowledgment of the courtesy the queen had shown to me.

I wasn't sure if I should thank her for it, for one wasn't supposed to address the queen unless it was in response to a specific question. But thanking her was the reason I was there, and since she was looking at me with slight but definite interest, I was about to speak when she asked, "So, cousin, is your new home to your liking?"

"Yes, Your Majesty, and I'm here today to thank you for having provided the means for me to have it. Thank you."

"Yes," she replied, pausing. In the brief silence, I looked up at her face. She seemed not to age as others did, and although now almost forty, she looked at least five years younger. The features which gave her beauty — her thick red hair and green eyes — were still the primary things one saw, and with the help of garments and jewellery, detracted from what wasn't perfect.

"You have only to ask if you find your pension insufficient," she went on simply, but at the same time somehow wordlessly conveying the startling message that she respected me for what I'd done. Instead of thinking I'd wanted to marry for love or security, she'd known it had been to try to have a child who could become king or queen. Even though her response had been one of anger, I believed that she knew it was something she might have done herself, had our positions been reversed.

"Thank you," I said again. Suddenly, I felt sympathy for her. I'd been able to marry while she was too frightened to, because she was queen.

She looked away, towards the courtiers she'd been speaking to before, and I saw the audience was over. "Don't bother with the curtsey; it can't be easy for you," she said. "And turn around and walk out naturally. Don't try that backward walking — you might fall, and everyone looks ridiculous doing it, anyway." To Mrs. Parry, who'd already stepped back to my side, she said, "You neither. Go — leave me to deal with these fools again." The returning courtiers must have heard her, but I'd already turned around and couldn't see their response.

"And so, it's done!" Mrs. Parry said as soon as we were back in the outer room, and had moved apart from the others, none of whom showed us any interest at all. "A short but very successful audience. It seems she even likes you a little, now. She was different with you than with any of these others out here when they go in to speak with her."

"She can afford to be. It's a different game being played now from when I saw her last. Only if I married and had a child would I be in it. But I won't do that or anything else political. She's satisfied I'll spend the rest of my life in my little house on Minories Street. And that's what I intend to do."

"You'll be welcomed at all the festivities, wherever the queen is."

"I doubt I'm going to go. None of these courtiers are going to have any interest in me."

But as if to contradict me, at that moment the Countess of Lennox left the group gathered around her and walked over to us. "Cousin," she said in greeting, which I repeated. I waited to find out what she could possibly want of me, but she merely continued to look at me. Behind her, Charles had taken her place in the centre of the little group that had gathered around them, and seemed to be holding his own in the conversation with them. Then, I understood she was using me as a reason to give him the opportunity to do exactly what he was doing, letting the others see he was becoming someone to be reckoned with.

"My condolences on the loss of your husband and son," I told her. "And congratulations on being the grandmother of a king."

"Yes," she replied, instead of thanking me. "James is already a better king than his mother ever was a queen. A foolish, foolish woman, Mary Stuart is. She was a queen of France and a queen of Scotland, and who knows what might have followed here? But it's over for her now. The Scots don't want her back. The best she can do is to try and stay on Elizabeth's good side, so that her son can succeed her. But that's something I doubt she can do. It's not in her nature. Not a good queen, and not a good woman. She murdered my son, you know."

"I was told that. I'm sorry. He didn't deserve it. He had his life before him."

She stared at me. "He died knowing his son would be a king," she then said resolutely. What I'd surmised had been correct, that in the end, she thought it had been a price worth paying for her grandson to reach the throne. She also likely thought her husband's death had been worth the regency to stabilise their grandson's reign in his crucial first years of Scottish politics.

No one besides Mrs. Parry was near us, and I knew she'd never repeat it when I then said to the countess, "You're going to win, aren't you? It's going to be one of your descendants who wins this game of succession, no matter how many years away it is. But make no mistake: it's not going to be because of your skill, but because the queen decided it."

Beside me, I heard Mrs. Parry take a quick breath, surprised I would say such a thing. But the countess's response was smooth. "A lovely thing to say, Lady Mary, and one I thank you for." And with that, she turned and swept back towards her son.

"My goodness, she liked what you told her!" Mrs. Parry said.

"She'll never change. I didn't expect her to agree, of course, although you can see that she does. But I had to say it."

Although I intended to return to the city that same day, I had to wait until the afternoon for the tide to change. Mrs. Parry had already told me I could do so in her room, and dine there, if I wanted to. I accepted her offer.

Her room was larger and nicer than many of the others at Windsor Castle, and her serving woman made me comfortable in it, bringing me pillows and a blanket for the bed so I could rest comfortably. I was even able to sleep before the food Mrs. Parry had sent was brought in by the servant, who then took the used dishes away. A short while later there was a knock on the door. Opening it, I saw Lord Henry Seymour.

After he'd stepped in and the door was closed, he said, "Mrs. Parry told me you'd seen the queen today, and were waiting here for the tide. And she said that her servant was off on some errand, so we'd be able to speak if I wanted to. I do. I'm sure you want to hear how your nephews are."

He was past thirty now, and looked more set in figure and steadier in manner, although still not middle-aged. Thomas had told me he was good-natured and liked by everyone, when they'd both participated in the tournament a few months after we'd met. His position as a courtier and agent and representative for his brother the earl appeared to have continued successfully during the years since then.

"First," he began, "let me say how sorry I am about the death of your sister. She died too early."

"Twenty-seven. My age right now."

"Like I said, too early. Although it would've been a loss for us at any age. She was grieved not only by Ned and their son, but by my mother and sisters and brother. We asked to be allowed to attend her funeral, but the queen wouldn't allow it for any of us. Ned particularly wanted to go; he petitioned the queen, but she didn't even respond to it, the same way she'd ignored his requests to visit Catherine after he'd learned her death was becoming imminent. The one kind thing that the queen did was have our younger nephew sent immediately afterward to Hanworth Place. He was five at the time." He waited for a moment, as though preparing to say something that would affect me, then added, "His name is Thomas."

"Thomas," I repeated. "That was my husband's name."

"Yes, I know, the sergeant porter. A very fine gentleman. We were all pleased when he was allowed to return to Lewisham, and then became Captain of Sandgate Castle. But we think that happened because the queen needed him to have things running properly there. She's always capable of seeing what might bring the best results, and adjusting her personal feelings accordingly. Although Catherine died hated by her, the queen seems to feel my brother might be useful in the future, and so he's been allowed to return to Hanworth, and has recently been shown some small favour. But she still refuses to acknowledge our nephews as rightful successors despite many other people thinking they are, especially those in the Reformed party. Even so, she knows they are being educated as though that might eventually come to pass one day, and she hasn't objected to it. My family thinks she might change her mind about them eventually. Either one of them could become king."

He seemed to expect that I'd respond with approval, but I didn't. As it stood now, Catherine's children would have futures of their own, separate from the royal family, and ones that might be more fulfilling for them. The quest for a throne would likely bring misfortune to them, especially if they were made to pursue it without wanting it themselves. Besides, I didn't think it would be possible. "It won't happen," I said quietly. "Even with the support of the Reformers, the political situation has changed now. The young King of Scotland is being taught the Reformed religion, and the Countess of Lennox has had her second son educated so as well. I spoke with her today, only briefly, but long enough to see her determination for Elizabeth's throne to pass to one of her descendants."

"My brother is determined also," Lord Henry said, "since the death of Catherine." But he spoke a little uncertainly, as though he might agree with me but didn't want to say it.

"I suppose you've no way of knowing how she felt about him?" I asked. "In her final year, did she love him?" I looked away, not wanting him to see that the question had been prompted by my uncertainty over how Thomas may have felt about me at the end.

"A few days before the end, Catherine asked one of her servants to let Ned know he could be certain her love for him was a great comfort to her as she departed this life for the next one," Lord Henry answered. "It was several months before the servant was able to get to Hanworth to tell him, but she eventually did. It gave him peace of mind. It was then that he became resolved to see one of her children on the throne. No matter how things stand politically right now, they can change. Mary Stuart would need a Catholic foreign army to help her take the English throne, and France and Spain don't have the resources for such an enterprise in the near future, especially with no help from Scotland, which is Reformed. The Earl of

Huntington — who you must have seen here today, full of self-importance as the new President of the Council of the North — is ageing, and his claim as a champion of the Reformers has already diminished beside the claim of Mary Stuart and Darnley's son. The future may go differently for the King of Scotland, or our nephews. It's a long way off. Meanwhile, the only other person with a claim to the throne is you. Have you any desire to pursue it?"

"Look at me. No one has ever thought me suitable. I don't look the way a queen should."

"Stranger things have happened. A party could form around you."

For the briefest of moments, the possibility of it stayed in my thoughts. The Earl of Hertford had wealth beyond most earls, as did his mother, currently the country's only duchess. With that, and wise political strategy, a party could be created around my claim to follow Elizabeth, with two nephews to follow me. A vision of the future stability of the country would be presented that could appeal to everyone, Catholic or Reformed, with no hint of foreign involvement. And although reaching the throne myself would still be unlikely, I'd have the satisfaction of seeing a nephew as king, or set to become so. But in the next instant, I was certain that if the Earl of Hertford was intent on such a dream, he would have to pursue it without my participation.

Lord Henry then asked if I would like to visit our nephews at Hanworth Place. "None of us knew you're now living in your own house. I only found out today when Mrs. Parry told me. When I tell Ned and the others, I think they may want Edward and Thomas to meet their mother's sister. Do you think the queen would object?"

"She understands I have no ambitions, political or otherwise, except to live quietly and make a life for myself at my new home. I do want to meet them, but the visit should wait for a while. And perhaps it would be best to have them brought to where I'm living, instead of my going to Hanworth Place. I have a small house on Minories Street, not far from the Aldgate." When I met them, I wanted them to see me in an everyday setting, as it was for most people.

Our conversation was done. As Lord Henry left, I thanked him for having sought me out.

A while later, on the Thames in the wherry bringing me back to London, I thought about what he'd said. His offer of help from his family had been sincere, and I knew that I could rely on them if I needed to. But my becoming involved politically was something I didn't want. The most significant thing he'd told me had been how at the end of Catherine's life, she'd loved the earl.

When we approached the city, Westminster Palace came into view, with Whitehall beyond it. On the way to Windsor that morning I'd barely even seen them, since I'd been readying myself for my audience with the queen. But with that behind me, my thoughts now went to Thomas, especially as we neared the Water Gate. The last time I'd seen him had been right inside it, in the waiting gallery, before I'd left with the queen. That day, everything had been as we'd wanted and planned, and we'd had hope of a life together before us. The wherry was close enough for me to see the outside of the window he'd been standing beside. I could picture the way he'd looked then, taking the time to speak with me, though it had been such a busy day with many people waiting for him.

The wherry moved on, the window disappeared from view, and then we were passing the steps to the water. Today, the steps were empty, with no barges or wherries at them, as there seldom were when the queen wasn't in residence. We moved past, and a moment later the Water Gate was behind us, leaving me with the image of those empty steps. I suddenly felt a loss deeper than any I had yet. Soon after the last time I'd seen him, Thomas had no longer been sergeant porter. It seemed impossible that by the end of his life he could have felt anything but regret for ever having met me. But it was something I had to know the answer to.

14

The next morning, when I came downstairs, I called Henry Goldwell in from the kitchen and told him I wanted to go to Lewisham the next day. "I'd like you to accompany me, if you don't mind doing so."

"Lady Mary, it's what I'm here for. Yesterday I felt I should have gone with you to Windsor, but it wasn't my place to say so."

"There was no need for it; that was a trip I was familiar with. This isn't. I'm not even sure where the place I want to go to is. We'll need to take a wherry to Deptford, and there hire a wagon to go out to Lewisham. But I can't drive it myself, so I need you. It shouldn't be more than a mile and a half. I'm thinking that in Deptford someone should know the exact destination."

I could tell he was interested in why I was making the trip, but didn't want to ask. I offered, "It's the home of my deceased husband's family. I want to visit them."

His expression changed, as though he instantly understood I hadn't reached the decision easily. I continued, "It's so close to Deptford they'll be known there. I've met all of them before, his brother and sister and children, not only when Mr. Keyes and I were married, but some during an earlier visit they made to Whitehall. Your aunt was such a good friend, helping me organise the dinner for them that day. She helped me with so many things."

"Anne and I both hope to continue to do so. I'll be ready to leave at whatever time you are tomorrow."

He went back into the kitchen to get my breakfast. Although the door was closed, I could hear him in conversation with Anne, who was likely being told of the trip. A few minutes later, when he returned with a tray with the dishes, she followed him in. Although I saw him give her a look that indicated she should go back, she ignored it. As I took my place at the table and he set out the dishes from the tray, she stood with her dark eyes fixed on me, as though she wanted to say something.

"Lady Mary…" she finally began.

"Anne," Henry said, arranging the dishes before me, "Lady Mary makes her own decisions."

"What do you want to say, Anne?" I asked.

"Henry tells me he's going with you to the Keyes family's home tomorrow. I think I should go too. Can I?"

"Yes, of course. I'll be grateful for the company. But Anne, why?"

"For you. I want to be there if it's disturbing for you. Henry doesn't always understand how things can affect someone, and I can be of more comfort if you need it. Going there in your circumstances wouldn't be easy for anyone. Are you sure you want to? You've barely spoken of Mr. Keyes since we've been here, and I thought it must have been because it was too difficult for you to. And now, all at once, you decide to go out to Lewisham. Lady Mary, you don't know how Mr. Keyes' family feels about you now, and you may not be received as you should. And even if you are, you'll feel his absence from that house. I don't think you should go. And if Henry's Aunt Frances was still here, she might tell you the same!"

"Anne, you shouldn't —" Henry began, but I stopped him.

"No, Henry, please. Anne is only saying things I've thought myself. And I appreciate that she cares enough to say them."

To her, I said, "It's not going to be easy. You're right about Thomas's family — I've no idea what they think about me now. They might prefer if they never saw me again. But I've never been to the house, so I don't expect his not being there to affect me like the Water Gate did yesterday, when I passed it. It was almost impossible to think that someone else was sergeant porter there now. I know I could never go through that gate again! If I ever need to go to Whitehall Palace, I'll have to go by land to one of the other entrances. But the house in Lewisham isn't the same."

"Wouldn't it be best to write first, to see if they'd mind if you visit?" Anne asked. "At least then you'd know you're welcome. It would make it a little easier for you."

Henry, holding the now empty tray, stepped back from the table, saying nothing, but exhaling in such a way as to show he thought she'd said enough. But I said, "You're very thoughtful, Anne, and you see much. Yes, of course, it would at least be polite for me to write first for an invitation. But this is something I realised yesterday that I have to do. Thomas — Mr. Keyes — and I intended that to be our home, and we'd planned to eventually have many fine years together in it. I feel I have to see it now, even only once. I have to walk around it, and hopefully set in my thoughts that it was a dream worth having, and one that almost came true. That's something that for the rest of my life I can hold on to. But if I wrote and they replied that I shouldn't visit, I don't think I could go anyway. No, best for me to go unexpected, no matter the reception I receive."

"I think they'll be kind to you," Henry said.

"I hope so. There's also something I have to ask when I'm there, if I feel any of them might know the answer."

*

Our wherryman perfectly navigated us around the many ships anchored in the Thames at Deptford, where the Royal Dockyard was located. The crowded dock and streets leading from it felt new and strange to me, with everyone seemingly full of shipbuilding expertise and hurrying about in very determined ways. The conversations taking place around us, and orders and directions being given, were filled with all types of technical terms I didn't understand. Wagons with freight I didn't recognise were being packed in front of storehouses, and in the background was the constant sound of purposeful work.

We found the tavern we'd been directed to at the dock, which we'd been told would have a wagon for hire. Inside, Anne and I waited while Henry spoke to the proprietor, a distance away from us in the main room, almost empty at this time in the early afternoon. At first, there seemed to be some sort of issue, but whatever it was passed, and I saw Henry pay him from the money I'd given him. Then the proprietor went into another room, and Henry returned to us.

"He wanted us to take his own driver, because he thought I might not return the wagon," he explained. "But once he heard where we were going, he changed. He said very respectful things about Mr. Keyes. Everyone here knows the family, it seems. And they're at the house; some of them were seen in Deptford earlier this week." He hesitated, then said, "He knows who you are. I didn't say yes or no, but after the mention of Mr. Keyes, he knew."

It wasn't difficult for me to understand that my condition had been the reason why. That he knew how I looked was interesting, but I couldn't tell if it was a good sign or not for how I might be received at the house. "Thank you for telling me," I said.

"He asked if we wanted a coach instead of the wagon, saying he could find one. But I said no, the wagon would do. He gave me exact directions to the house."

The proprietor reappeared at the door he'd gone through, and called for us to follow him, which we did, through the kitchen to the yard where the wagon was. He bowed low as I passed him, saying again he could get a coach if I wanted to wait. But I thanked him and said the wagon would be sufficient.

On the road to Lewisham, the landscape very quickly changed to one of open meadows on both sides, a serene contrast to the streets of Deptford. The day was fine and the air was sweet with the scent of the autumn countryside, and as the wagon rolled along with me seated beside Henry, and Anne perched behind us, our surroundings seemed to hold the promise of a successful conclusion to the visit. But I wouldn't allow myself to think so until it had happened.

The house became visible at the end of a long driveway, flanked by trees from which brown autumn leaves, stirred by a slight breeze, floated down onto us as we drove beneath. At the front door, the driveway widened, but continued down the house's length and around the corner, likely leading to less formal entrances and a barnyard. Henry stopped the wagon directly before the door, got out and came around to my side to help me down, saying, "After you go in, Anne and I should drive around to the back. We can wait for you there, unless they invite us in. But we're going to stay right here until that door opens and you're inside."

On the ground, it took a moment for me to adjust after the long ride, during which I looked at the house. It was beautiful, clearly centuries old, with many windows along its front, and the perfectly placed door like a centrepiece to welcome visitors.

I imagined Thomas standing there, waiting to receive guests the same way he had at Whitehall's Water Gate. But here there were no steps, the door opening level with the driveway, and before it was a long lawn, still mostly green, with a carpet of leaves bordering the driveway. It was the type of appealing family home anyone would want, and the thought that it had almost become mine followed, but I quickly pushed it away.

I went and knocked on the door, aware of Henry and Anne sitting behind me in the wagon, watching. The door was opened almost immediately by a tall older woman with grey hair, whose strong resemblance to Thomas instantly would have told me she was his sister, if I hadn't known already. I was taken aback, having expected a servant, a tiny delay before meeting the family, who'd have a moment to decide whether or not they wanted to see me.

Although Thomas's sister been at my wedding with her other brother and nephew, she at first didn't seem to know me. With little interest, she said, "I saw the wagon on the drive from the window. You should use the kitchen entrance for deliveries." She started to close the door.

"It's not a delivery. It's not why we're here. Why I'm here."

Her blue eyes were so like Thomas's, it was almost as though he was seeing me through them as recognition dawned. Before she could respond, someone in the house approached behind the door, and Thomas's oldest daughter stepped into view beside her.

Instantly, she knew who I was. "Lady Mary!" she cried in surprise. "Aunt, this is Lady Mary who married Father!"

She of course was seven years older than she'd been the last time I'd seen her, now a young woman in her early twenties. She curtsied, and her aunt did the same.

"Please, don't do that," I said, taking a step forward. I wished I knew their names, for it would have set them at ease. But I'd been told them at a time when I'd often forgotten them. I was different now, and saw others for who they were, not merely for how they related to me.

The aunt suddenly seemed to awaken from a dream. "How rude to keep you standing here!" she said as she opened the door more widely and gestured for me to enter. "Please, forgive me for thinking you were making a delivery!" Fortune then helped me, for she turned to her niece and said, "Isabel, go and tell Uncle Edward and Thomas that Lady Mary is here! Then get Anthony from his studies and Annie from the kitchen and bring them to the parlour. In the kitchen, tell cook to send in some of our best wine."

I silently rehearsed their names: Edward was Thomas's brother, Isabel and Thomas the older children, and Anthony and Anni the younger. Only Thomas's sister's name was left unknown, but a moment later I learned it when young Isabel, before going for the others, said, "Aunt Isabel, please take Lady Mary's cloak!"

"How foolish of me," she replied. "Please, let me have it!"

As young Isabel turned to leave, I said, "My servants are in the wagon out back. Could you please let them into the kitchen to wait? We've come by wherry on the river to Deptford, where we hired a wagon."

"Yes, certainly!" She turned and nearly ran through the house.

The older Isabel helped me out of my cloak, and placed in on a nearby chair. "Such a wonderful surprise," she said as she led me into the parlour. My anxiety over my reception vanished, for I saw that it would be the same with the others.

The parlour was wood-panelled and luxurious, with fine furniture. It was intended to be the best room in the house, but had signs of being used daily by the family. Chairs had comfortable-looking cushions and there were Turkish carpet coverings on tables. The front window had a chair and small table before it, with a needlepoint frame with fabric set on the table, as though someone had been at work on it. The view of the driveway from the window suggested it had been the older Isabel, who'd seen us approach while sitting there. Once, I thought, there had been the possibility of another chair on the other side of the table, where I would have sat with my own needlepoint frame.

There were sounds of a commotion elsewhere in the house, with doors opening and closing, and hurried footsteps. One by one, everyone appeared, all exclaiming with welcoming surprise upon seeing me, and gratitude that I was there. Anthony and Annie, now adolescents, were more reserved than the others, and looked at me as they would a stranger, but with frank and open interest. I knew that at their age, the years since they'd seen me would have seemed longer.

The older Isabel asked if I would stay for supper, or even overnight, but I said no to both. Perhaps there would be time for other visits later, but today had been too full of emotion, and I knew I'd need time alone to settle it. "No, thank you, we must go back today. I have my own house on Minories Street now, and I have responsibilities there. I planned this as a short visit. I wasn't sure where this house was, or if any of you would be here." I looked away from all of them, to the parlour door I'd entered through. "Or if so, if you'd want to see me."

There were immediate declarations that I shouldn't have felt so, giving me reassurance that if present, Thomas would have said the same. "I can't thank all of you enough!" I said, and felt the tears in my eyes.

They saw them and responded. A chair was pulled over to the other side of the table by the front window, right where I'd thought mine would have been, and I was guided to it, after which Edward sat in the one that earlier his sister had been in. If things had been different, it might have been Thomas and I sitting side by side. For the briefest moment, I half closed my eyes and thought it was so.

Young Isabel said she'd go for the wine and hurried out, while her brothers brought forward a bench and chairs from around the parlour and set them closer in front of me. When they all sat down, it easily could have been any afternoon visit where they'd gathered for me to entertain them with some story. But today it would be for one, or all, of them to tell the story that I was there for.

Isabel returned carrying a tray with a pitcher of wine and cups, which she set on a table and poured, giving a cup to each of us. "Your servants are comfortable in the kitchen," she then told me, before I could ask after them again.

She took a seat next to her aunt. Then there was a moment of silence, during which the house seemed a peaceful haven that could have been deep in the countryside. I said, "It's difficult to think we're so close to the city here. And even closer to Deptford, and all the ships."

Edward said, "A ship from there took Thomas's remains on it. He was buried at sea on its way to the Continent."

I turned to look at him, so surprised I nearly spilled my wine. My face showed my question, which he'd clearly anticipated.

"An unusual request," he continued, "but he made it in his final days while still clear in mind. It was the water he loved, whether the sea by Sandgate, or the river near here at Deptford or by the Water Gate at Whitehall. The sea, he said, would flow into the Thames, and on to the Water Gate. We could then think of him whenever we saw it."

No one was drinking their wine, either holding their full cups or placing them on tables, which I now did with mine. Steadily, I said, "He had depths to him that I'd only been starting to see. For me, his burial is especially fitting. The last time I saw him was right inside the Water Gate." I was about to cry again, but was able to stop it. But I couldn't stop myself from saying, "I regret his position being taken from him because of me!"

Again, they all immediately replied with expressions of comfort. But it was Thomas's son who then said clearly, "You must never feel that way. Never. My father never regretted marrying you, not once. He spent his final years after he'd returned here still trying to have the marriage accepted."

The older Isabel said, "He told us he'd learned that you'd refused to blame him for it, as the queen wanted you to do. He said it was the kind of person you were. Most people would have saved themselves. He also told us he'd offered to have the marriage undone, if possible, but only for your benefit. He said his concern had been what might follow for you. He told us all of this; he wanted to make sure that his children followed his example —— and yours — of how others should be treated."

"And he loved you," Edward said. "I never asked it, but one day near the end he told me. He said at first, you'd both planned to marry for ambition, to have a child who could take the throne after the queen. But that changed, he said, and by the time you married he loved you. At that same time, he said that although he wished it had turned out differently, he had no regrets."

A silence followed, with only an occasional sound as the breeze outside blew a few stray leaves against the window. It felt as though Thomas, unseen, was somehow still alive and there in the parlour with us. Although the house hadn't become mine, it was enough for me to know that it was here. And I knew that even though they'd all be pleased if I returned, I never would again after today. They'd been kind and gracious, but I wouldn't pretend they'd become my family, or ask them to. Something had now been concluded. I'd got what I'd needed to from the visit, beyond what I'd hoped for, and I could now go back to my new life on Minories Street.

We then spoke of other things. They told me more about Thomas's death and what the year preceding had been like for him, then moved on to the marriage plans for young Thomas and young Isabel, the scholarly education of their younger siblings in recent months, and the adjustments made by Edward and his sister after the death of their brother, in anticipation of the new spouses of their nephew and niece entering the household. When it was time for me to leave, the older Isabel brought my cloak and helped me into it with all the care she might have given to any family member.

"We'd like for you to return," she then said, when we were a little apart from the others. "But you're not going to, are you?"

"No," I answered. "I don't belong here. Thomas would understand." She said nothing, but I saw she understood as well.

They all accompanied me through a side door to the back yard, where Henry and Anne were waiting with the wagon in the wide space between the house and the barn. Henry started to get down to help me in, but Edward stopped him, saying he would, and started bringing me around to the other side. We were almost there when suddenly there was the sound of a barking dog. I looked around to see one running across the yard towards us.

"Here, Prince!" Anthony called out to him. He was a greyhound, sleek and full of life and eager to be with the family. Each patted his head, before he ran over to where I was with Edward, who greeted him also. Then, he stopped and sat down in front of me, as though waiting for acknowledgement.

An odd feeling of familiarity came over me. Then, staring down at the dog's handsome grey eyes, I knew that I'd met him before. He was the puppy I'd encountered years ago, the one who'd once belonged to Lord Darnley. I remembered that Thomas had promised me that the dog would have a good home with his family.

"Did you know I was the one who brought the dog to Thomas?" I asked. "And that he was given to me by Lord Darnley?"

The family replied that they hadn't; Thomas had never told them of Prince's earlier owner. No one could remember how his name had been chosen either, other than that Thomas had left the decision to them.

I didn't tell Henry and Anne of Thomas's burial at sea until we were in the wherry on the Thames, the wagon left back at the tavern we'd got it from. Anne made no comment, but Henry said thoughtfully, "It's the water of the river, and the sea beyond, which brings us from one place to another — always more easily than by land. The palace Water Gate is going to be there for centuries."

A few minutes later, Anne said, "A beautiful dog, that Prince was."

"I was thinking it might be nice for us to have one in the house," I said. "There's already a yard for him. Henry, do you think you could find a puppy?"

"Certainly. Should I start looking for one tomorrow?"

"Yes," I told him. "Tomorrow." And the wherry continued, bringing me towards my new home on Minories Street.

HISTORICAL NOTE

Mary lived in the house on Minories Street for the rest of her life, which continued for another five years. Records show her participating in the New Year's exchange of gifts with the queen, an indication that she remained in favour. When she died in 1578, she was buried in Westminster Abbey.

A NOTE TO THE READER

Dear Reader,

Thank you for reading *The Queen's Game*, the fifth in my series of novels about the Tudor and Stuart succession. Whereas the last two books dealt with descendants of King Henry the Eighth's older sister Margaret, this one's narrator, Lady Mary Grey, is from the same branch of the Tudor family as central characters from the first two books, descended from Henry's younger sister Mary. Like its predecessors, it continues the story of the family struggle for the eventual succession to the throne of what is increasingly apparent is to be a childless queen, against the backdrop of the ongoing religious conflicts of the time.

The Queen's Game is a novel, and not intended to present a full biographical portrait. My choices are always to select and creatively develop a particular strand, or perhaps a related few, of the many that make up a person's lifetime, that can fit within the structure of a novel. For this series, as I've stated elsewhere, those have been stories of royal women whose ambitions played out through their children, or their desires and ability to have them.

Mary Grey has over the years been presented by writers of both fiction and nonfiction, but for me her primary motivations always remained elusive. So, I suppose it was inevitable that I would eventually offer my own suggestions as to what those could have been. As always, I have stayed within the range of facts available. I should mention, though, that I have placed the Water Gate at Whitehall rather than Westminster Palace, where it is usually described as being. This decision was based on the possibility of 'the Water Gate at Westminster' referring to the neighboring Whitehall Palace, which was also located in Westminster. Factual descriptions of Thomas's duties, and others of the gate, also seemed to fit better with the less official and more residential use of Whitehall. And so, my choice to place it there.

There is a wealth of biographical information about my subjects available on the internet, and I would encourage anyone seeking more knowledge about them to pursue their interest there. If you do, you'll find I have adhered to all reliable facts, especially dates and places. If you encounter any apparent difference, I suggest you search deeper, the way I have, into other sources.

I am always grateful for the interest of my readers, and enjoy reading their comments. If you liked *The Queen's Game*, or any of the other novels in the series, I hope you'll post a review on **Amazon** and **Goodreads**.

Thank you!

Raymond Wemmlinger

Sapere Books is an exciting new publisher of brilliant fiction and popular history.

To find out more about our latest releases and our monthly bargain books visit our website:
saperebooks.com